THE GIRL IN CABIN
B54

THE
GIRL IN
CABIN
B54 ∿

by LUCILLE
FLETCHER

F/ELE

NEW YORK ∿

RANDOM HOUSE

THE GIRL IN CABIN B54

1

IT WAS a hot July morning in New York City. Haze lay over the leaden harbor. Aboard the S.S. *Columbia*, high on her top deck, Dr. Vernon Grove gazed upward at the steel teeth, the glittering jawbone of the skyscrapers grinning above all the thousands of sweaty victims they had just swallowed up and would soon disgorge for the noon lunch hour. The sky was the color of chlorine.

Dressed in crisp summer whites, braided cuffs gleaming gold on the ship's rail, Dr. Grove might easily have graced a royal yacht rather than this old slow-going ocean liner. His face was fair in coloring, handsome, set off by a coat of tan. His tall figure was upright and trim. His cap was set at a jaunty angle, his brass buttons twinkled. Many a sweating longshoreman, gazing up from the ropes or the mounds of heavy luggage on the pier below, might have envied him—or hated his guts.

He was the ship's chief surgeon. At the moment he had little to do. But the *Columbia* could not sail at noon without him. He was well aware of this as he glanced down at the toiling crew and the passengers swarming up the gangplank in the midsummer heat. They were all potential patients, all 543 of them, a thought that gave him little joy.

Squinting impatiently at the portside parapet, where a junior officer was awaiting sailing instructions, he turned his eyes again to the city he was once more about to leave. There it lay, sweltering—old, familiar, hideous New York—grinning its inhuman grin. He despised it, hated the very dust of it, which even now was sifting down on his immaculate white uniform and settling upon the filth-laden harbor. But at the same time its brazen towers and its fetid streets had the power to reduce him to the dimensions of a waxen figure on a wedding cake, to shatter his aplomb.

There, up to the north, lay Columbia's P. and S., one of the finest medical schools in the country, where he had graduated twelve years ago in the top ten of his class. To the east lay Bellevue Hospital, where he had interned—and met his wife. There, beyond the haze, in laboratories, in operating rooms, men no older and no smarter than himself were hard at work this morning, performing research, fighting cancer, opening brains and lungs—while he, at thirty-six, was drifting like that watermelon rind in the sluggish water, lapping at the hull of this white ship.

Eight years! And that made how many voyages? He couldn't count them. Eight years—of running like a starched white rabbit around this tub—and meanwhile, what had it gotten him? Loss of his wife, loss of his son, and something far more harrowing. As usual, whenever he faced his life with complete honesty, Vernon Grove began to sweat.

"All ashore that's going ashore . . ." The first warning gong was sounding.

Up the gangplank they were still coming—all the fat old women and the dull old men. All who were afraid to fly, or who looked upon the *Columbia* as a fun house, Bali-Hai at sea. There were old maids wearing drip-dry suits, with orchids pinned hopefully to their bosoms; wolves who were giving every woman the eye; babes in arms and honeymooners; spry crones with hectic flushes on their cheeks and anxious relatives in tow. July was always a madhouse—of suburbia. But here and there he also spied a pretty face or two—a giggling trio of college girls, a couple of chic little private secretaries, who had obviously saved all year for this vacation, bought new wardrobes, made their reservations months in advance.

Standing now in a roofed section of the mezzanine deck, Vernon Grove surveyed this brand-new crop and appraised the possibilities.

A sensational late-comer! His roving eye was caught by a truly marvelous head of hair, copper-red, waist-length, straight out of color television. It belonged to a thin pale Vassar type in a madras shift, who was sauntering up the First Class gangplank, carrying an armload of books and magazines. Behind her was a tall, gaunt, elderly woman, dressed in gray, who kept plucking at her arm and shoving her along. He observed the girl with waning interest. She was not only chaperoned, she looked far too young and above it all for the Fun and Games of the *Columbia*.

The two swinging blondes going past him now, in white miniskirts and peroxided falls, were definitely not above it all. Undulating sexily through the throng, their every smile, their every movement was a come-on.

"Seven Carefree Days at Sea. Relax in Luxury. Every Night Is a Fiesta." So read the company advertising (in desperate competition with the jets). And those little blondes, with their wig boxes and false eyelashes, were ready to conform to the image. So was that tall dark chap in the turban who was eying them. So were a number of husbands, whose wives were looking very restless. And so, as a matter of fact, was Vernon Grove.

He smiled faintly. He was beginning to feel more cheerful. There was a certain lift and excitement in these last few moments of departure, inevitably.

They might even be starlets, or chorus girls from some Broadway show—though celebrities were few and far between aboard the S.S. *Columbia*. None was listed for this crossing. "You must meet *so* many famous people," his mother often remarked loyally—from her wheel chair in the nursing home. But he didn't. Real celebrities, the top-drawer kind, preferred the jets, or those much faster, bigger, smarter ocean liners that got across the ocean in four days and didn't overemphasize the cruise atmosphere. All the *Columbia* got, for the most part, even in First Class, were the middle-brows, and it was rare that he ever had anything more exciting at his table for seven in the Wedgwood Room, supposedly composed of V.I.P's, than department-store executives, small-factory owners, lawyers or the military—with their wives, who were, invariably, withered.

The final gong began to shiver through the noise and the babble. The ship's orchestra struck up. Long looping streamers of confetti drifted through the humid air. And now, suddenly, a woman wedged herself in next to him. She gripped the rail with polished fingernails, and stood looking down over the side, her face transfixed.

She was a brunette and elegant in an expensive-looking white suit. Petite and slender, she had that special patina which only money and taste can give a woman. Her hair was darkly sleek and fashionably styled. Her profile was a cameo. She was the right age, possibly around thirty.

The doctor was impressed.

What or whom she was looking at with such intensity he couldn't tell. The people on shore were moving and surging in a body now to the open end of the long pier, where in a huge multicolored lump they would soon congregate to cheer and wave a last farewell. The doctor glanced at her sidelong. She was gorgeous.

The whistle sounded a long deafening blast. The gangplank was removed, hawsers were cast off, and the tugs began to puff into action.

"Leaving someone?" A lousy opening, and he wished he had it back. He smiled and jauntily touched his cap. "I'm Dr. Grove, the ship's doctor. Welcome aboard."

The woman turned her head, staring at him vaguely.

"Welcome aboard," he repeated uneasily.

"Thank you." Her tone was cool. "Yes, I'm leaving my husband down there . . ." Her voice trailed off. She began waving again.

He nodded gravely, but he did not move away. He remained there to sustain her at this moment of crisis.

Ignoring his presence, she kept staring out over the side. By now they were being nudged away from the pier. A widening band of dirty green water was opening. The watermelon rind bobbed and went under, disappearing for good. Hands began to wave from the pier like sheaves of wheat, and cheers arose as the great ship swung ponderously into position to head downstream. Even after eight years these maneuvers could still fascinate him. There was majesty and drama in the way the *Columbia* was being handled. Like a great white queen she moved with dignity, the envy of all eyes on shore.

He looked again at the woman beside him. He tried to pick out her husband back there on the pier, but could only imagine him, cramped and sweating in a hot suit, squashed into that mob of flies, straining his eyes for her—the unlucky slob.

He felt a tap on his shoulder, and turned to confront the chief purser, Bob Jenkins.

"Vernon, I've been looking all over for you. Have you heard about Gary?" He motioned the doctor away from the rail a few steps, and addressed him in low tones.

"Gary? No. What's with Gary?" Gary, formally known as Dr. Gary Brightwood, was the assistant surgeon.

"He's quit. Jumped ship. His mother phoned in about fifteen minutes ago and said that he was fed up with his job. Isn't that a hell of a note?"

"God!"

Vernon Grove had never particularly liked Brightwood, a pompous kid not long out of medical school. "Fed up with the job, eh? Well, I'll be damned. Did the exec get me anybody else?"

"How could Anderson get anybody?" the purser replied. "At fifteen minutes before sailing time? He's sore as hell, of course, but the company said to go ahead. Do you think that you can manage it alone?"

"What else is there?" Glumly the doctor looked out toward the receding city, then back over the throngs on board. "We've sailed, haven't we?"

"Can you?"

"What else?"

The purser vanished. Dr. Grove moved thoughtfully back to the rail.

The great harbor, hazy, filled with traffic, was opening before them. Past the bland face of the old green Statue of Liberty, through the Narrows, under the high span of the Verrazano Bridge, the ship moved on steadily, like a stately swan. The flag at her stern began to flutter. A cool breeze swept her decks, where the passengers were still jamming the rails, waving to the crews of the tugs, waving to a passing freighter, thrilled and excited by the sight of the diminishing shoreline and the haunting music of the bell buoys. Dr. Grove still lingered in the fresh air, next to the brunette lady, watching her reactions. She had the look of someone who was leaving all known things behind. She kept twisting the diamond ring on her left hand. Ahead stretched a waste of blue— lonely, limitless.

"Are you from New York?" he ventured finally. "Is this your first trip on the *Columbia?*"

Yes, she was. *It* was. Her name was Mrs. Edward Harrison. She was still aloof, vaguely distracted. She had been to Europe several times, last year, in fact. She and her husband had gone over aboard the *United States.*

"Oh, I think you'll like the *Columbia* much better," Dr. Grove assured her, smiling. He had removed his cap, and the wind was tossing his thick sun-bleached hair. "We're slower, of course, but we do more things."

"Like what?" She smiled.

"Like—well, masquerades, ship's concerts, talent shows. It's corny, of course, but that way you get to know people, and we have to kill time somehow for a week." His blue eyes danced. His tall frame lounged beside her boyishly at the rail. "Are you an actress, Mrs. Harrison, by any chance? You look so—well—like Gina Lollobrigida. You aren't? Do you sing then? Dance? Play any kind of instrument? I'm supposed to rake up talent for our show on Sunday . . ."

"Me? I'm afraid not." She was smiling and blushing. "I'm afraid I haven't a single accomplishment." She lowered her eyes. "Will you excuse me, please? I have some unpacking to do. But it's been so nice, delightful."

"Enjoy your voyage, Mrs. Harrison."

"*Thank* you."

She went swaying down the deck in very high heels. Her legs were beautiful, the skirt was very snug, and the wind kept molding it. This was going to be a very pleasant crossing. He was looking forward to it very much.

2

ONCE OFF Ambrose Lightship, the great sea took over. The wind picked up and the motion of the ship became her own. She was a swan no longer. She became a gull, breasting heavier swells, and a raw salty breeze blew across her decks and cooled her stuffy corridors. Hatches were slammed shut, gates were locked between the classes, a tightening process set in as the fine veteran engines began to thunder. And there began all those hundreds of assorted noises which the ship's passengers would hear for the next seven days: the groan and grind of the engines, the heavy rhythmic thump of the propellers, the rattle and tinkle of metal on metal, creaking sounds and straining sounds, all produced by the force and conflict of a mighty object driving through wind and wave, blending into the unique percussive music of a ship at sea.

Nodding to passing stewards and stewardesses, side-stepping steamer trunks still awaiting distribution, Vernon Grove hastened below to his quarters on A deck, and unlocked the door. "VERNON GROVE, M.D., Chief Surgeon, Hours 2:00 to 6:00 P.M." said the sign thereon, and beneath it there was a smaller placard. "GARY BRIGHTWOOD, M.D., Assistant Surgeon." He removed the latter, dropped it into a wastebasket.

His quarters comprised a waiting room, a larger examining room, and a private stateroom with bath, all very spacious, nicely furnished, and kept immaculate by his efficient room steward. The sun poured in on waxed linoleum, wall-to-wall carpeting, and polished paneling. His equipment was modern and his drug cabinet well stocked. Below decks, the *Columbia* also boasted a small but well-equipped hospital bay, which contained four beds, and an operating room with complete facilities. She was, medically, a very up-to-date ship—thanks to him.

He peeled off his white uniform, changed to the regulation navy-blues worn at sea, and settled down, glad to be back in the routine again, glad his damned three-day shore leave was over, glad to be off.

Born in Brooklyn, he had grown up with the smell of salt, the presence of the ocean. As a boy he had lain in bed in his mother's tiny Bay Ridge apartment, listening to the music of the foghorns on a misty night. On Sundays he had walked along Shore Road with her and watched the ships steaming by through the Narrows.

Eight years ago, stepping aboard the *Columbia* for the very first time on a sticky June day, saying to his wife, "Just for the summer, Peg . . . just to earn a little money for the kid and you"—he had felt an instantaneous, secret, overwhelming ache. He could not wait for the engines to start. His heart at twenty-eight had been that of a cabin boy, and this, he knew, had been his wife's undoing, not the women (at least at first), or his refusal to accept responsibility, or that he was sick and tired of doing everything expected of him, but simply this: this crazy thrill of excitement, this empathy that he was feeling now.

He had come to know and love every aspect of the North Atlantic: the languorous smoothness of a summer calm, the eerie beauty of a day of fog, the passion of a fierce northeaster, for in the past eight years this doughty old vessel had withstood all weathers, splendidly. And if there was one voyage he looked back on with horror, with a chill running up his spine, it was long ago, nearly two years ago, and something never to think about again. This was July of 1966, and they were under way again for a week of glorious adventure.

His nurses were arriving.

"Come in, girls . . ." In they came—three-strong, white-uniformed, registered, hospital-crisp. Young Miss Murphy from Cleveland, Mrs. Levy from Pittsburgh, Miss Simmons from Rutland, Vermont. They all looked very nice, fresh and rested, happy to be back, and of course they were all agog and dying to discuss the flagrancy of Dr. Brightwood. "Did you hear his excuse, Doctor?" Norma Murphy giggled. "Fed up with his job?" Yes, he'd heard. The words still pricked his ego. "That's what his *mother* said," he told them. "She telephoned." "Now isn't that disgusting?" Mrs. Levy sniffed, sticking another pin into her elaborate blond coiffure. "Hiding behind Momma. What a schlemiel." But Miss Simmons, who was the oldest, painfully plain, and had been here the longest, clucked her tongue and sighed. "But it's terribly unfair to *you*, Doctor. Now you'll never get a moment's rest."

"Oh—I'll manage," he said.

"You'll be on call twenty-four hours. Day and *night*."

"I don't plan to do a lick," he said. "I'll leave it all to you."

They giggled.

The responsibility, nonetheless, was huge. The ship was now an island for a week, and if they ran into bad weather or some kind of epidemic broke out, he'd be a wreck long before they reached Le Havre. But he preferred not to worry about such things right now, and actually, except for the inevitable seasick cases and digestive upsets, there was often not enough work to keep the staff occupied. This crowd looked pretty healthy too.

After lunch (a martini and a club sandwich served in his cabin) his phone began ringing with the usual complaints.

People had drunk too much champagne at their seeing-off parties. They were overexcited. They had overeaten of the smorgasbord at lunch this afternoon. And now, unaccustomed to the motion of the ship, though there was still not much of a sea, they were drooping in their cabins, ringing bells and squealing. Dr. Grove moved briskly about, dispensing good cheer and Dramamine. To many, as he stepped over the threshold, with his fair hair shining and his blue eyes twinkling, he must have seemed a figure out of television. "You remind me *so* much of Dr. Kildare." Many a woman had said that.

He kidded his patients. He needled them. "What? You think this rolling is bad? Wait until we really get going. Why, it's like a lake today." And the passengers loved it. The old ladies tittered and looked braver immediately. The children ceased to whine. "Like a lollipop, Buster? Can you keep *this* down?" He always carried a supply of suckers in his medical bag. He passed out compliments on floral arrangements and bulging fruit baskets. "See you in the lounge *tonight*, Mr. Smith." Or Mr. Jones. Or Mrs. Tannenbaum. Or whatever. It was the kind of bedside manner he'd be ashamed to have the guys back in medical school see. But it worked, nine cases out of ten, so what the hell.

Besides, this job wasn't all pandering to rich slobs, because he also had the crew members to treat. He stewed in miserable cubicles as well, handled dirty bodies stacked up in bunks.

There had been plenty of near-fatal accidents in eight years—knife cuts, burns, and guys losing fingers and toes in the machinery. And they liked him, too, the oilers, the electricians, the deck hands. "Hey, Doc. Gracias, señor." He could speak a little Spanish, a little Norwegian, Polish and French, and could sling the four-letter words around in at least three other languages.

But he could only hope that everyone below and above decks would stay healthy for the seven days of this crossing. For, Brightwood or no Brightwood, he had every intention of enjoying himself—as usual. Even if he had to cut a few corners, burn the candle at both ends, life for Vernon Grove aboard the *Columbia* could never be all work and no play.

To shower and shave, to dress in a fresh uniform, to saunter like a king into the gilded main lounge, the Wedgwood Room or the ship's movies, these were his rewards and his prerogatives. To sit and chat with people in dinner jackets and cocktail frocks, people aglow, people euphoric, was to feel himself euphoric and aglow. He was respected and admired—in any strata of the ship's society. He was hailed with joy and listened to with hushed fascination. After all, there were certain social requirements to this job, one of which was to make the passengers feel at home; as a single man and a ship's officer, he was expected to be extra polite to wallflowers, ladies who might be feeling rather lonely on board. There were all those V.I.P's at his table he was also supposed to entertain. There was the Talent Show, the Masquerade Party, where he always helped with the judging. It was unthinkable to ignore these aspects. People found his company stimulating. It was an honor just to be chosen to sit with him. "We have the ship's *doctor* at *our* table . . ." He had often heard that phrase in breathless tones.

Then, of course, there were the women.

For instance, there was Mrs. Harrison.

The subject of women aboard an ocean liner might make a very nice piece some day for the A.M.A. *Journal.* Such amazing things happened to the female sex on an ocean cruise. The sea air acted like an aphrodisiac. Or maybe it was the motion. Or the carnival atmosphere. Whatever it was, and he had never seen it otherwise, the ladies, married or single, young or old, simply went to pieces aboard the S.S. *Columbia.* They toppled like tenpins—into bed. They melted at a glance. And as an officer, a good-looking man, a young man with a healthy appetite, he had distinct advantages.

As he had come to know the moods of the Atlantic Ocean, so in the past eight years Vernon Grove had come to know many phases of womankind. And he had never known failure. There had been furtive but feckless housewives, sportive debutantes, chic career women, corn-fed maidens, expert foreigners. He had learned their foibles, and compared their flesh—like a connoisseur. In the past eight years it had become a Collection. It had become a Game. In the last two years it had become an indispensable form of therapy.

And the best thing about it was that once the ship docked, everything was over, called off, wound up. In Le Havre, or nearing Southampton, the lady simply folded up her tents, tucked her lust back into her suitcase, and silently stole away. She went tripping down the gangplank, never to be seen or heard from again.

In all these eight years there had been only one exception . . .

"How are things going, Harry?" Dim lights were on, dim music was playing, as he stood beside the bar in the main lounge that first night out, sipping Scotch. The best. Dirt cheap. It was 1:00 P.M., and he had told Miss Murphy he was to be called only for the most dire emergency.

"Pretty good, Doc. Fair. The usual crumbs." Harry was the First Class bartender, a Sicilian, with very shallow, reptilian eyes. "Say, I heard about your friend Brightwood jumping ship. What was his story?"

"He was no friend of mine. His mother phoned and said he was fed up with his job." He was getting damned bored with talking about Brightwood and his stupid excuse.

"Yeah? His mother?" Harry snickered.

Wasn't Mrs. Harrison a First Class passenger? Or wasn't she the drinking type? Dr. Grove's eyes scanned the crowd on the dance floor, and those drinking at the onyx-topped tables.

"That kid was crazy about his job," Harry was saying. "He loved it here, just as much as you do, Doc . . ."

Maybe Mrs. Harrison was still determined to miss Mr. Harrison. She was lying in her cabin, perhaps, undressed, shedding lonely tears. Or writing the old man a letter, which could not be mailed for the next six days.

"Say, you looking for those *twins*, the blondes, maybe?" Harry was asking. "They're over there, behind the pillar."

"What blondes?"

"The *mod* blondes. The babes from Carnaby Street."

Harry leered at him, and for no reason the leer, the reference disturbed him. He felt a sudden sharp twinge of uneasiness.

"Or is it that brunette?" Harry grinned. "With the big brown eyes. And the dress down to here? She was *asking* for you."

"Me? I don't believe it. Are you serious?" His twinge of uneasiness began to abate.

"Is her name Mrs. Harrison?"

"Yes."

"Oho. So you know her *name* already." Harry chuckled. His swarthy face was wreathed in benevolence again. "Well, she was in here, at the cocktail hour, and she drinks vodka martinis, and she says to me, 'You have a veddy *nice* doctor on this ship, veddy good-looking, veddy kind. What's his name again?' So—I told her Gary Brightwood, naturally."

They had a couple more laughs together, and he drank two more Scotches. He felt warmed and convivial, even euphoric, by eleven o'clock. He even danced with a couple of homely older women, to do his duty by the *Columbia* and to prove to Harry that he wasn't interested in blondes from Carnaby Street. Then he retired below, stopping off to see Miss Murphy, who was still on duty.

"Any calls, Nora?"

"Not a thing. It's been silent as the grave," she said. She seemed itchy, and he knew the reason why. She had a date, the minute Mrs. Levy relieved her at one o'clock, with the chief dining-room steward, Phil Doyle, a married man with four kids. Miss Murphy happened to be engaged to an accountant in Akron. But "c'est la vie" aboard the S.S. *Columbia*. The sea was the sea. And Nora Murphy, with her carrot hair, her fresh, scrubbed look, had succumbed like all the other single girls.

"I'll take your calls until Mrs. Levy comes." He smiled at her tolerantly. And she grinned back gratefully, scurried off in her thick white shoes.

As he undressed in his cabin that night, his eyes met the eyes of John Vernon Grove, Jr., aged nine, a picture sent to him dutifully the previous Christmas. The eyes were very blue, very clear, the eyes of a handsome little boy with a cocky smile. He was looking at his own face—almost. There was the same superficial air of optimism, the fair good looks.

He felt a surge of affection, a wrench of sadness. This past Sunday's visit had been hell, sheer hell. He had jolted in a hot crowded train all the way up to that remote fashionable hamlet in Connecticut, spent a fortune in taxis, and all just to see the kid for an hour and a half, most of which they had spent looking at the toys, the bicycle, the rabbits and the other junk that "Daddy George" had bought.

The house, the grounds had been deserted. Margaret, her second husband, the recent baby had fled the scene, leaving only Johnny and a sullen maid to confront the "monster." And how self-conscious, how forcedly polite the poor kid had been. They had strolled up to the village drugstore to buy a couple of ice cream cones. Johnny had been embarrassed all the way. And in the store, the old druggist had made it worse. "How's your daddy, the doctor, sonny? How's your momma? How's the baby sister?" Utterly ignoring the tall stranger with the boy, blind to any resemblance, the old fool had kept plying the child with questions, while the poor kid scuffed his shoe and stammered out pathetic answers. It wasn't worth it. It was hell on the kid. He would never submit him to a similar ordeal, never put up with such an arrangement again.

In the stillness of his cabin on the North Atlantic, he sighed. To hell with Margaret, and her ideas of stability and custody and Dr. Spock and what a husband and father was supposed to be. It was *she* who had left him, and *she* who had remarried, and now it was he who had to pay the penalty. He had been perfectly willing, seven years ago, to let the marriage remain intact. But no, she had wanted a stuffed shirt, and she had gotten one. So had little Johnny. "Daddy

George," the big fat internist from Park Avenue, was giving him everything he was supposed to have. He was going to a private school. He was eating his Wheaties. He was playing in the Little League. But, God, thought Vernon Grove, gazing at the photograph, he looks like me, I fathered him, he's mine, the only thing I have.

And how they'd love to take him away from me. They'd jump at any excuse at all for me never to see him.

As he stood there, a trickle of fear, icy fear, went curling up his spine.

Finally he crawled into bed, pulled the covers up, but it was quite a while before sleep came. And then the mighty rhythm of the ocean cradled him. The ship plowed on through darkness.

3

HE COULD not have been asleep for more than a couple of hours when his bedside phone rang. It was Mrs. Levy. "I'm sorry, Dr. Grove, but there's a woman in First Class who insists you come to see her niece."

"What seems to be the trouble?" It was twenty minutes of two.

"I can't make it out exactly," Mrs. Levy replied. "She has an accent, and sounds kind of old and deaf. But it sounds as though the kid is having hysterics or something. They're in B54, Doctor, and the name is Stewart."

"Okay."

Night calls had always been Brightwood's responsibility, damn him, but there was no getting out of this one tonight. A First Class passenger was a V.I.P., and he wasn't any Park Avenue internist who could tell his patients to make an appointment a week from now. Dazedly, hauling himself from bed, he began to dress. It was only after he had dashed cold water on his face that the cabin number really registered.

B54.

Someone old and deaf, with an accent. With a kid. A child.

He checked his supply of lollipops. Frowning, he left his office.

A kid with hysterics.

The corridors at this hour were gloomy and deserted. No ribaldry. The bars, the lounges were shut down for the night. He met no one as he passed the rows of closed cabin doors, went down the rubber treads of the companionway. He heard no sounds, except the creaks of the old hull and the steady pounding of the engines. The *Columbia* was still straining along through plenty of wind.

Cabin B54 was a small double stateroom, one of the cheaper First Class accommodations, and it was set off by itself at the end of a narrow cul-de-sac. The children's playroom flanked it on one side, a women's shower on the other. It had privacy of a very special kind—and isolation. He had not been near it for the past two years.

For a moment, standing at the entrance of that dimly lit corridor with its familiar gray steel walls, he felt a wave of panic. Then striding forward resolutely, he rapped on the steel door.

The door swung open immediately. A tall, gaunt, gray-haired woman, wearing glasses, was standing there in the dim light, smiling at him vaguely.

"I'm the ship's doctor. Mrs. Stewart?" he asked.

"No. I am Mrs. *Graham*. My *niece* is named Stewart." Her voice was low, precise, vaguely British, quavery. Clutching her lavender bathrobe tighter about her bony frame, she turned. "I'm so sorry to disturb you at this hour, Dr. Grove."

"It's perfectly all right, ma'am." With one swift, almost covert glance he eyed the familiar tan rug, the cramped dingy atmosphere of Cabin B54. It was dimly lit, cluttered with women's clothes. The only light was at the head of one of the twin beds, where his patient was lying.

And his patient was no child. She was the languid Vassar type he had noticed earlier, at sailing time, strolling up the

First Class gangplank with this same tall elderly woman. The girl with the marvelous red hair.

"Ellen dear, the doctor has arrived."

On the twin bed against the wall, she lay limp and wan. The coppery hair, great masses of it, streamed out over the pillow, swirled about slim shoulders in a high-necked nightdress. Her eyes were shut. Her breathing was shallow.

"Miss Stewart? Ellen?" He touched the slender hand lying limp on the brown blanket. "What's the trouble, Ellen?"

She opened her eyes for a moment and looked at him. They were startling eyes, greenish blue, very large, very clear, and they illumined her pale face with a strange, unearthly beauty. Wide-eyed, unsmiling, she gazed up at him blankly, and for a moment he was looking at some antique goddess, some being from another world. Then just as suddenly the feeling passed. She was just a kid, a rather pretty, washed-out-looking kid.

"Hello, Ellen," he heard himself saying. "What's wrong with you?"

Her eyes closed.

"Ellen, dear . . ." Mrs. Graham had withdrawn to a corner, where she fidgeted nervously. "The doctor is here to *help* you."

The girl lay silent.

"What's been going on?" He turned to the aunt. "My nurse said something about hysterics?"

"She had a nightmare," the old woman answered in low tones. "It frightened her. She woke up screaming. Then she seemed to lose consciousness."

"Over a dream?" He frowned.

"Yes." She nodded, blinked her eyes behind their thick old-fashioned spectacles.

"How old is your niece?"

"Nineteen. Almost twenty."

"Has she had other seizures of this type? Does she suffer from any kind of nervous disorder?"

"No!" The dark eyes stared at him. Then the old woman shook her head emphatically. "Ellen has always been healthy, very healthy," she said. "It was just the dream."

"I see. Well, let's take her temperature." After he had placed the thermometer between the girl's pale lips, he asked, "You folks are English?"

"No. Well, my niece isn't. I am Scottish, Doctor. Ellen is from Virginia. Her parents are dead. *Both* dead." Speaking now barely above a whisper, she kept glancing nervously at the girl. "I came over to the States about three months ago to look after her, after her father died. I'm from Edinburgh. That's my home. I'm taking her back with me for a wee visit, till she has to return to college."

"Where does she go to college?"

"Sweet Briar."

"Sweet Briar? That's in Virginia, isn't it? I hear that it's a very excellent school."

Still the girl had not stirred or said a word. He withdrew the thermometer. Her temperature was normal. "I'd like to listen to her heart, Mrs. Graham. Can you undo the nightgown?"

"*I'll* do it."

Still not opening her eyes, his patient had blurted out the sentence in a soft, choked voice. And the sound was somehow a relief.

With one swift gesture she raised her hand to the blue ribbon at the throat of her white muslin gown and jerked the ribbon loose.

Applying the stethoscope to the soft white flesh underneath

the nightgown, he was aware of a very well-developed body, in spite of his earlier impression of almost boyish slenderness. His earlier impression had been wrong.

"Your heart sounds perfect, Ellen."

"I could have . . . um . . . um . . . told you . . . um . . . that."

Dr. Grove raised his eyebrows.

"Ellen has some trouble with her speech, Doctor," Mrs. Graham said in an embarrassed whisper. "It's particularly bad when she's upset like this. At other times you might not even notice it."

"Oh." Dr. Grove swallowed. Then he smiled sympathetically. "Well, don't be upset with me, Ellen. I'm just the kindly old ship's doctor. Okay?"

There was at last the flicker of a smile. She opened her eyes again, and all over again he felt the same shock at their beauty, their uncanny magnetism.

"I'm not up . . . um . . . um . . ." Touching her throat and turning her head, she began gulping, fighting for articulation. He had observed speech defects of this type before, but they were not very common. In one less self-conscious (less of a perfectionist?) the defect would have taken the form of a machine-gun-like stutter, and blocked by the word "upset," she would simply have blurted out "ups-s-ss-" until she got it out. But Ellen, as if refusing to admit her flaw, merely froze, and kept gulping and gulping in the apparent hope that the blocked syllable or the entire phrase would be set free.

The spectacle affected him. On a sudden absurd impulse, he reached into his bag. "Like a lollipop?" he asked.

Her eyes sparkled and she began to laugh. "*Thank* you!" Color swept into her face. "You must think I'm an awful . . .

um . . . baby." Removing the cellophane, she studied the lollipop and then touched it delicately with her tongue. "And I . . . I suppose I . . . I am."

"Do you feel better now?" Dr. Grove asked.

She nodded. With the enormous blue-green eyes she cast him a shy look of gratitude.

"It was just a nightmare, a plain old nightmare, right?"

She nodded. "Yes . . . except much . . . um . . . worse. More . . . um . . . um . . . detailed."

"Everybody has a nightmare now and then, Ellen," he said. "After all, you're in a strange bed, the first night out."

"Y—yes. But not . . . um . . . not like mine."

"What makes yours so different?" He smiled.

She rose from her pillows, the long hair lifting silkily around her, hair that glistened in the lamp's steady glow with such gleams and burnished highlights, it was like something separate from her thin pale face, like something with a separate life.

"I . . . um . . . um . . . *see* things."

"See things?"

"My niece, Ellen, believes that she is psychic." Mrs. Graham spoke in her low voice from the shadows. "She believes in ESP, what we in Scotland call the second sight."

"It's not just . . . um . . . a *belief*, Aunt Victoria," Ellen interrupted sharply. "It *is*. It um . . . um . . . *happens*."

"Yes, yes, yes, dear . . . but we mustn't dwell on it so much. The doctor isn't interested."

"You . . . um . . . aren't?" Ellen asked.

Dr. Grove smiled quickly. "Why don't you just let me give you a sedative, Ellen, something that will let you sleep? It's very late, after all. And we'll talk about it some more in the morning, if you like. Okay?"

The girl did not answer. She merely raised those strange green eyes to him, fixing her gaze upon him steadily, and again he had the feeling that this kid, this child, was looking deep into him, almost past him, beyond him.

The ship shuddered with a heavy swell. Metal clanked against metal in the adjoining bathroom, and the brass handle of the porthole rattled. Through the glass oval of the pane he could see fields of whitecaps on the ocean, constantly forming, constantly dying, like a million ping-pong balls tossed by the dark cold sea.

His heart had suddenly begun to pound. It made no sense. It was entirely due to Cabin B54. But suddenly he couldn't wait to get away from these two staring strangers. He felt as though he could not breathe.

"Well . . . !" Frantically he thrust his hand into his bag, fished out a couple of tranquilizers, and slapped them down on the built-in dresser. Sidling toward the door, he said, "Those will help her, ma'am—in half a glass of water. Now both of you try to get some rest, please. Just relax, and forget about that nightmare, miss."

"Thank you very much for coming, Doctor," Mrs. Graham said. She made no further attempt to detain him. Soundlessly she glided to the door and opened it. At the threshold she thanked him once again with her strange vacant smile. "We do so appreciate it, at this hour . . ."

But Ellen Stewart said nothing at all to him. Glancing back, he saw her sitting up in bed, studying the lollipop. And then the door was closed. He was alone, once more, on the deserted creaking ship.

4

ABOARD THE S.S. COLUMBIA, *July 9th, 1966*

8:00–9:30 A.M. Breakfast, Wedgwood Room
10:30 A.M. Conga Lessons, Main Lounge
                 Bridge in the Smoking Room
11:00 A.M. Bouillon Served on Deck. Pingpong,
                 Shuffleboard
11:30–1:30 A.M. Swimming Pool, First Class Hours

STANDING BEFORE the bulletin board the following morning, Vernon Grove also noted that at six o'clock that evening there would be a cocktail-mixer for all First Class passengers, and that the evening's movie was a first-run film, starring an actress who had recently come into prominence.

Life was normal and routine. Life was on an even keel again. The sun was shining brightly. The winds of yesterday had calmed. The seas were level as a lake. The ship was gliding smoothly.

Refreshed by a few hours of sleep, he felt more like himself. In the light of the morning, under a cold shower, he had already decided that his reactions to Miss Stewart and her aunt were absurd, an illusion brought on by his weariness and the lateness of the hour. The girl was a teen-aged neurotic who had been upset by unfamiliar surroundings, and she was obviously spoiled. Her aunt was old and ineffectual. He would just forget them both, avoid them, and if they phoned again, he would turn them over to his nurses from now on.

With determined zest he headed down for the First Class dining room and breakfast.

Two boys in uniform manned the leather doors. They greeted him respectfully.

"Good morning, Dr. Grove."

"Good morning, Joe. Good morning, Al. Nice day." Returning the greeting with a gracious smile, he paused on the threshold in his handsome dark blue uniform, a striking figure of a man.

The Wedgwood Room was all that its name implied—cool, green, formal, elegant, with touches of white. It had recently been redecorated and air-conditioned. Its many portholes filled it with light, and the sea looked into it through a dozen eyes. Often the ocean's gaze matched the walls and the carpeting, but on this brilliant July morning the sea was a deep rich blue. They were passing through the Gulf Stream.

Neither Mrs. Graham nor her niece was visible.

Mrs. Harrison, however, was.

With her sleek dark head outlined against the blue horizon, her slender figure clad in pink today, she was seated at a table a goodly distance from the doors, surrounded by three middle-aged women in drab cardigans—like a rose amidst a patch of briars, he thought. She was sipping coffee, looking pensive.

Setting a circuitous course, he zigzagged through the tables casually, a bemused look on his face, and when, as if by accident, he found himself passing her group, he looked at her, then looked again, faked a double-take, smiled, and said "Good *morning*."

"Good *morning*, Dr. Grove."

She blushed, looked flustered, looked quite clearly pleased. She had remembered his last name.

But he kept on going. This was the Game, a game that he had learned to play, in the past eight years, with a subtle sense of timing, pace, gradual movement, escalation. These were the rules he had set for himself—with full awareness, of course, that the voyage lasted barely a week.

By now his course had brought him to his own table, where he must face the six V.I.P.'s whom Doyle had assigned him. And here they were, four of them so far. Two places were still empty.

"Good morning."

Four faces looked up at him curiously. Then everybody smiled.

"I'm Vernon Grove, the ship's doctor."

The burly male in the sports shirt was already on his feet, extending a hand. "Bob Ewing, Doctor." His hand was wrung. "And this is my wife, Judy. And meet Father O'Connor, Mr. Aziz. Mr. Aziz is from Iraq, on his way back to Basra. Great little town, Basra." Ewing had a florid face, a hearty chuckle.

The tall dark man with the turban flashed very white teeth; he was the same man who'd been eying the two blondes yesterday. The priest beamed on him pontifically. Mrs. Ewing was a plain little woman of middle age, with a sharp pointed face and a girlish air. She wore her brown hair in bangs. Simpering, she plunged immediately into small talk, as though it were her task, not his, to make everybody feel at home.

"We just adore your ship. It's so comfortable. Bob and I have never crossed on it before. We usually fly, but we wanted to be leisurely. Isn't the weather divine?"

As she chattered, he appraised the others, who sat looking

him over, saying little. Gradually he was able to collect a few details, none of which explained why they had been selected to sit with him. Ordinarily he was supposed to have a few of the elite, and Doyle was usually meticulous. In this new crop, he was surprised to find very little that could be called outstanding.

Father O'Connor seemed to be no more than an ordinary priest from a Jesuit seminary in Astoria, Queens. Large and powerfully built, he had a New Yorker's accent and a fleshy Irish face. Aziz, whose appearance was ageless, had just been studying at the University of Michigan. "The course for engineer—I *like*." His English was primitive. Ewing was merely an army major, retired. He and Mrs. Ewing lived in Florida, in a Fort Lauderdale condominium.

Philip Doyle was slipping.

However, dutifully, politely, Dr. Grove struggled on. "And where are you bound for, Father O'Connor?" he asked, toying with his eggs. "Are you getting off in Le Havre or Southampton?"

"Southampton," said the Jesuit. "I am on my way to London," he added importantly, in his flat Brooklyn accent, "to attend a conference, yes, a pretty interesting affair." He nodded his big cropped gray head, and rustled in the black silk cassock.

"Really? What is it about?"

"Behavior. Stress patterns. My field in the Order, you see, happens to be psychology."

"Very interesting."

"Psychology?" Mrs. Ewing piped eagerly. She had been listening with her sharp face cocked. "Oh, I *do* think there's so much need *internationally* for *understanding* people in this day and age."

"Yes, indeed." The priest nodded.

"My husband and I, we *both* feel it's so important." She glanced at Aziz's dark face, and then addressed the doctor in earnest tones. "Everywhere we've been, and Bob and I of course have lived practically everywhere, we've done our best to understand the natives, Doctor. Tried to *live* like them. It's so important."

"Yes, it is," said Dr. Grove.

The atmosphere was awfully stiff.

He smiled at Mr. Aziz, who was looking dreamily at him through horn-rimmed spectacles.

"And where are *you* bound for, sir?"

"I—*theenk*—the Southampton. Eng-gland . . . yess. I go —maybe take short ride to Shakespeare cowntry—Stratford Avon?" He was pleased, delighted to be paid attention to at last. He rolled his big black eyes, he wriggled.

"Oh, you *know* about Shakespeare?" Mrs. Ewing asked.

"I *love!*" He placed his hand upon his striped brown vest. "Oh—tello . . . and the Taming of the Screws."

Major Ewing guffawed.

Mrs. Ewing frowned at him, and reddened.

Major Ewing began asking about their two missing table-mates. Squirming in his chair, and swiveling his balding head on its thick bronzed neck, he eyed the doorway repeatedly, and as each newcomer entered, nudged his wife. "Think they're the ones, honey?" Why he was so inordinately inter-ested, it was hard to determine, but perhaps having sized up the others he was a trifle disappointed in the prospects for mealtime gaiety . . . as was Vernon Grove.

"They're probably seasick," Dr. Grove suggested absently. He was again watching Mrs. Harrison far across the room. She had already drunk several cups of coffee, smoked several cigarettes, and was still dawdling at her table even though her companions had left. She sat in lonely melancholy, staring out at the sea, but once she turned her head and their eyes met for an instant. He had never seen a more wistful expression, a more dazzling smile.

"Yes, it *is* the Gulf Stream, Mrs. Ewing. The weather should be perfect."

After breakfast there was morning inspection. In a stiff parade, the ship's officers followed Mr. Anderson, the executive officer, around and around and up and down the decks. And maybe Anderson was inspecting the ship with a gimlet eye, but not Vernon Grove. For him this was a time to see and to be seen, a time for looking over the field once more and checking his original impressions.

Marching erectly, with jaw set gravely, he was the image of the stern, dignified young officer, but his blue eyes still managed to dance everywhere. The men slouching in their deck chairs glanced up with grudging interest and envy, the young people playing ping-pong paused and gawked and, like keys on a piano, one by one, the head of every woman on deck bobbed up in a long rippling arpeggio.

He saw neither Ellen nor her aunt anywhere.

Inspection *was* an impressive spectacle. It was good psychology for the passengers to see all these rugged men in blue sweeping by. It bolstered the fearful. It raised the morale. The ship, on this bright summer day, with the warm wind of the Gulf Stream blowing, moved like a huge white castle, well kept, well scrubbed, in excellent order from bow to stern. She cast a great gliding shadow on the blue ocean, a shadow flanked by the reflections of the puffy white clouds. To circle around her briskly that day was a pleasure, and Vernon

Grove, in his heart of hearts, felt enormous pride.

And Mrs. Harrison was clearly the pick of all the women—in First Class and otherwise. His instinct had been right. So she was Choice of the Week.

She was sitting in a deck chair near the stern of the promenade deck, very near the briskly spanking American flag, and he made a mental note of the exact location. Right after morning inspection he was supposed to inspect the ship's kitchens every day, but this morning he let this dull chore wait. Instead he went back to the promenade deck and started sauntering aft rather slowly. Sauntering was a very useful form of behavior, a technique of the Game.

Bouillon had been served by now, and certain questions went with the sauntering. He asked, "How is the bouillon?" Or "Not having any bouillon?" Or "Not having any crackers with your bouillon?"—all equally inane. Yet to so many of the ladies they might have been the most fascinating, thought-provoking questions ever asked. Such was the effect of his blue uniform, his lordly attention.

When he reached her chair at last, her book was closed on her lap and she was practically panting for him to notice her, lying back in a languorous pose, shading her fine dark eyes with a shaking hand.

"Hi!" He smiled down at her. "How was the bouillon? Not having any?"

"No. Should I? . . . I just adored your parade."

Next to her was a dough-faced woman who was also beaming at him greedily.

"Did you?" He laughed modestly—at them both. "It's routine, of course. It happens every day. You probably won't even notice it by the fourth day out. But"—squaring his shoulders, he looked toward the flag—"it *is* a safety factor, and I suppose good for the passengers' morale."

"Oh, it *is*," she said. "I think it's very reassuring." Sitting up, she swung her legs aside, and he caught a glimpse of lacy underwear. "Do you have time to sit down a minute?"

"Thank you. I would love to, Mrs. Harrison." He smiled a rueful smile. "But I'm afraid I'm swamped with patients today." He glanced at his watch. "Are you planning to attend the cocktail-mixer this evening?"

"Mixer?" exclaimed the dough-faced woman thirstily. She reared like a horse.

"I saw it on the bulletin board," Mrs. Harrison said. "Is it fun, Doctor?"

"Oh, it's fairly pleasant. You might enjoy it. It's a way to meet people, and there's dancing. The drinks are complimentary too." He smiled at both women, fixing his eyes on neither.

"And will *you* be there?" Mrs. Harrison asked.

"I'm *supposed* to be." He shrugged. Again assuming a dutiful air, he gazed meditatively at the flag. "But it's doubtful. I have a very, very full schedule.

Then, turning on his heel, he strode manfully away.

So *that* much was accomplished.

"Excellent! Great!" In the kitchens at last, he complimented the head chef, who was arranging truffles around a large cold salmon.

5

MAJOR ROBERT EWING looked up from his slab of cold salmon. His sunburned face creased into smiles. "Well, well, *well!*" He lunged to his feet, strangling his napkin, and thrust out a paw. "If this isn't a surprise. We've been a little short on *youth*—and—er—beauty."

Standing before them, looking demure in a sailor dress, was none other than Miss Ellen Stewart of Cabin B54. Alone. And she had obviously been assigned to this table.

Ewing jerked out a chair and blurted out the introductions. "Bob Ewing, my wife, Judy, Father O'Connor here, Mr. Aziz from Basra, Dr. Grove, our good ship's doctor . . ."

And she was smiling timidly at them all, her hand already at her throat, her throat convulsing.

"And what's *your* name, honey?" Ewing leered.

"Um . . . um . . ."

"Stewart." Controlling his chagrin, Dr. Grove stepped in for her. "Miss Ellen Stewart."

She darted him a quick look of gratitude and slid into her place, between Aziz and the major.

"Good afternoon, Ellen. Glad to have you."

But what the hell kind of V.I.P. was she?

He was relieved to see, however, that she looked considerably more normal today, girlish and well scrubbed. The fantastic red hair was smoothed back from her forehead and restrained by a black headband, from which it cascaded down her back in childish fashion. The sailor dress was simple and resembled a schoolgirl's uniform. She carried a white leather pocketbook. Nor were her eyes quite as overwhelming now. They were downcast and shy.

But of course, even so, she was a very striking spectacle—to these older types—and he could see that they were overwhelmed by her. Major Ewing was ignoring his salmon and looking positively fatuous. Twin spots of jealous color had begun to burn in Mrs. Ewing's cheeks. Even the priest was staring, sizing her up with masculine approval. And as for old Omar Aziz! His eyes were those of Ali Baba on the threshold of that treasure cave.

Open Sesame. Aziz sat bolt-upright, clearing his scrawny throat and fingering his tie. He rolled his bespectacled eyes heavenward, as though invoking some genie or other, rubbing some invisible lamp. Allah Akbar, the turbaned Arabian was obviously praying. Or recalling all the wiles of his forefathers which had lured many a succulent houri into a harem.

"You travels alone?" he at last ventured eagerly.

"No . . . um . . . I'm . . . um . . ."

"Ellen is traveling with her aunt." Vernon Grove again found himself supplying answers. "Mrs. Graham isn't coming in to lunch today?" he asked the girl.

"No . . . um . . . she . . . um . . . she is . . ."

"Seasick, eh?" Major Ewing was more than eager to help. And Ellen nodded gratefully, her face flooding with color.

Then Mrs. Ewing started asking questions. "Where are you folks from, dear?"

Ellen had tried to take refuge behind her huge tasseled menu, but dutifully she peered around it. "Um . . . um . . . Marshall, Virginia," she faltered painfully.

"*Marshall*, Virginia? Where is that, honey? I've never heard of Marshall. Have you, Bob?"

The child tried her best to be polite. She was at bay, surrounded by four staring strangers. And then the waiter came along, and she had to struggle through her order. Last night he had thought of her as spoiled, neurotic, certainly disturbing to be around. But today, seeing her blushing and stammering, gulping and suffering, he felt a twinge of pity. She had a cruel handicap, and it must have taken a good deal of courage to brave this table all by herself. Socially she was completely helpless, drowning in frustration.

Once the waiter had departed, shaking his head, Aziz, with many flashings of his teeth, started badgering her again. And panic overwhelmed her.

"You schools-girl, mees? You collitch students? Me . . . I attend the Universeety of Meechagan. Where you attend?"

"Ss . . . um . . . Sweet Briar."

"Svit Briars? Eees Meedle West?"

"Um . . . no." She made the effort to explain. Her face grew pinker and her eyes more desperate as she groped for words and sentences. A single syllable could hold her captive today, for the count of twenty—though last night, at times, she had spoken with fair fluency. Each phrase was like a mountain to climb.

"Svit Briars . . . Eees peeking flowerss?" persisted the idiot Arabian.

"No . . . um . . . not exactly."

He could bear this ridiculous ordeal no longer. No one else was helping her. They were simply looking embarrassed, or, like the major, trying to conceal a smile.

"Excuse me. Mr. Aziz!" Leaning forward, he interrupted the dialogue. "Did you ever in the course of your travels through Michigan visit Battle Creek?"

"Bat-tell Crick?" Aziz looked stunned. He shrugged and turned to Ellen again.

"Oh, but you must have heard of Battle Creek," Vernon Grove cried cheerfully. "It's not far from Ann Arbor, where you went to school. It's the city where they manufacture corn flakes. Cereal. Breakfast food. Ever eaten corn flakes, Mr. Aziz? No? You haven't? Honestly?"

Aziz sniffed. His eyes narrowed behind their spectacles. But Ellen's eyes began to shine.

"You must try them," Dr. Grove went on. "They're a real all-American dish. Oh, by the way, Mr. Aziz, did you know that I once had someone at this very table who ate corn flakes at every meal? *He* was from Battle Creek, Michigan, and he was the Kellogg's Corn Flakes Boy of 1929. Yes, a man of fifty. With a lot of freckles. He was quite a corn-flake eater."

He heard Ellen draw in her breath deeply. When he glanced at her, she looked the way she had when he had handed her the lollipop.

Aziz resembled a thundercloud.

But Dr. Grove went on talking, describing the Kellogg's Corn Flakes Boy of 1929 in minute detail. This man had never existed. He was making him up on the spot. Nor was Vernon Grove, by nature, a raconteur. But he had never rattled on so at random, in the course of his life . . . and why, he did not know.

"Every meal of his life, out of loyalty, I suppose, this fellow ate a bowl of corn flakes. Breakfast, lunch, and dinner, all were punctuated by a steady crunch." He faked another chuckle.

"Oh, how amusing. How adorable." Judy Ewing giggled. "Oh, Dr. Grove, what a perfectly fascinating life you must have lived." She was getting even with her husband for ogling Ellen all this time.

"Occasionally, Mrs. Ewing."

"Tell us all about it . . ."

"Yes," said Ellen softly. She was now looking totally relaxed. Her eyes were resting on him with a sweet strange brilliance. "I should love to hear about your life, Doctor . . ." And the words flowed smoothly. "Your life aboard this ship."

He excused himself soon afterward. He had the feeling that he had made a fool of himself—somehow. They all had, all of them. But he had barely gotten through the leather doors when he realized that she was right behind him. She had followed him out of the dining room, and was moving fleetly, faltering his name.

"Dr. Grove . . . um . . . Doctor . . ."

He paused. He faced her. Breathless and flustered, with pink cheeks and timid eyes, she stood before him in the sailor dress.

"I forgot to . . . um . . . thank you."

"Thank me? For what, Ellen?"

"For . . . for last night. And . . . um . . . today. You were terribly sweet to help me, um . . . um . . . with all those . . . strangers just now. And I do appreciate it."

"Think nothing of it."

"Oh, but I *do*. And . . . um . . . today, I'm feeling so much better. Those . . . um . . . pills worked . . . um miracles . . . and I'd like to give you this."

She unsnapped her white purse and produced a long thick envelope. She proffered it shyly.

He assumed it was a fee, and shook his head. "That's okay,

Ellen. There wasn't any charge. My services come free with your ticket."

She grew pinker and more flustered. "It isn't . . . um . . . money. It's some *writing*. It's . . . um . . . a letter I wrote you."

"A letter? What about?"

She pressed it into his hand. "Please don't open it immediately. Just . . . um . . . um . . . read it at your l-leisure, when you have the . . . um . . . time." For an instant the huge grave eyes regarded him. Then she hurried off.

Her long red hair hung down her back, swaying gracefully, and she swung the pocketbook. She was just a kid in a starched white sailor dress, with slender legs and flat-heeled shoes. Why she should upset him so, he could not fathom. But she upset him. Even here, in the light of day, in the sunny corridor, with people around, Ellen Stewart from Marshall, Virginia, had the power to disturb him.

He pocketed the letter.

He postponed reading it.

He was torn, actually, between the strong desire to open it at once and get the damned thing over with, and the just-as-strong impulse to toss it into a wastebasket. But the latter was impossible. As a doctor and a ship's officer, it was his duty to remain polite and do his best to please the passengers. Particularly the First Class ones. Meanwhile, it was almost two o'clock by then, and time for his office hours. He would read it later—after her peculiar influence had worn off. He would read it that evening, after he had had a couple of drinks. He would read it when he felt like it, "at his leisure," just as she had suggested.

So the afternoon went by.

He had a rather crowded waiting room that day, and was

kept so busy that he barely managed to change his clothes, shave, and get up to the cocktail-mixer by six fifteen. There, sure enough, was Mrs. Harrison, charming in a white beaded dress and delighted to see him. He had a vodka martini with her, and then another. They danced. She told him that her first name was Amy. "After the girl in *Little Women.* Isn't that old-fashioned?" She laughed, her dark eyes sparkling. "What's *your* first name, Doctor?" She'd been married for about six years, and her husband was a stock broker, ten years older than she.

"I *do* like the *Columbia.* It's so much more informal . . ."

She accepted his invitation to attend the evening's movie.

At eight o'clock—having forgone dinner, sharing a sandwich with her in the lounge instead—he parted with her briefly and went down to change his shirt and take a short siesta until the movie began at nine forty-five. He stretched out on his bunk. Tranquilized by vodka, and stimulated by success, he knew that he had at last achieved the proper state of mind to tackle something unpleasant. He felt the necessary golden edge, the fine glib haze.

So he took Ellen's letter from the bureau drawer and slit it open.

Lying back in the light of his bed lamp, he even found himself smiling at his own concern. Who was she, anyway, but some little Southern kid from some hick town in Virginia? It was probably a mash note. After all, she was a female, and this was the sea.

He began to read.

6

CONFRONTING him were four pages of sleazy ship's stationery, covered on both sides with neat schoolgirl penmanship, a clear round hand:

Dear Dr. Grove,

After you left our cabin, I couldn't go to sleep, so I'm propped up in bed, writing this to you at four o'clock in the morning. Aunt Victoria is sound asleep in the other bed. I feel I ought to write you some kind of explanation for my behavior tonight, since I realize that you might have thought it odd. It was impossible for me to express myself tonight at all, and I know that even if I try tomorrow I won't be able to, because of my speech problem. So writing is the only way to let you know in detail what kind of strange experience I had this evening, this so-called "nightmare," and maybe you can shed some light on it for me.

MY DREAM.

I dreamed tonight that I was dead. I have had death dreams in the past, but never quite like this one. The dream (or vision) took barely a few minutes. I wasn't really asleep, ever. In fact, I had just lain down on this bed when, almost as though some invisible hand had turned a television dial, the pictures, the sensations began. They were horrible, grotesque, a sort of filmed series of jerky sequences, lit by ghastly, flickering light, totally silent, a kind of "show" that I was looking at, involved in too, but altogether helpless to control.

I was dead. I was lying on my back in a coffin. I was stiff and motionless, as though someone had glued me into place. On my body was a long white satin dress. Perhaps it was some kind of shroud. I have never owned or even seen such a garment. But the worst of it was that I could see my feet, the points of my satin shoes turned up. Around my head something tight was wrapped, like a turban, or a bandage, pressing tight.

Vernon Grove sat up, feeling cold suddenly.

My face, my lips, my hands felt made out of stone. I knew that I was at my own funeral . . .
I could see an altar with a white lace cloth, and white candles burning. A man whose face I have never seen before was standing before me, with his head bowed, praying. Above me stretched dark smoky beams and ornaments of stone, the roof of some ancient church, and a bird was fluttering high up in its high stone arches. I wanted to scream, rise up and prove I was alive, like that trapped bird. I wanted to let the bird free and myself free.

The cabin was very still. The sea was very calm tonight—with an almost deathlike calm, as though the wind were about to change.

Then something clicked or snapped, and I was standing in the aisle of that old chapel, a part of the crowd. I was part of a group of mourners, grim, silent men and women dressed in black, and I was looking toward the girl in the open coffin, the girl in the white satin dress. I could see her quite clearly. She had golden hair, she was slender and young, a girl I don't know, have never seen before. Her face was suntanned below the white bandage, a face not beautiful but strong and sensual, a face so eager and so avid for life. With her beautiful golden tan, her voluptuous full mouth, she was lying in a casket now, like a doll dressed in satin, and I pitied her.

Vernon Grove's feet hit the floor, and for a moment or two he was tempted to read no more, simply tear this letter into pieces. But there were two more pages. Eyes glued to the childish handwriting, he read on.

I felt the most unreasonable, agonizing rage, a choking horror, and the desire to scream at all the people there, tell them to do something, stop staring at her. I can't express my frenzy as I turned from one solemn mourner to the next, standing there, unmoved, in rows, and then I seemed to be back in the coffin suddenly. I was again the girl.

The coffin lid slowly descended over me. I could see the stern faces of the men who were lowering it, blotting me from the candles and the fluttering bird and the pointed roof. Horror filled my soul, and now, with every ounce of my strength, I tried to move, to raise my head. I tried to open my mouth and scream. But my mouth was stuffed with cotton. And underneath me, like the swaying of a cradle, the coffin was beginning to move. Feet were shuffling, bodies brushed the wood. I could see both outside and inside that casket simultaneously. The images grew faster, sharper and more terrifying.

I could see the pallbearers carrying the coffin down the aisle of the church past the crowds of people. I could see the doors of the church opening, and the rain beyond, and the hearse waiting at the foot of the stone steps. But I was also *within* that dark satin-lined box, my body swaying, jolted, carried along, my heart shrieking soundlessly with terror, rage that my beautiful body, my young lovely body, was going to be lowered into a grave forever, smothered under cold dark earth.

I was sobbing and beating the air with my fists, Aunt Victoria says, when I came to myself finally—or rather, the images finally stopped. Came to myself? That is not quite true, for the spell this nightmare had cast was so strong, so powerful that it lasted even while you were here, Dr. Grove, and long after you had left. I was not myself tonight. Seldom have I ever been affected so by any form of psychic phenomena.

Can you give me some idea of the people who might have lived in this cabin before us? I am curious to find out. I have a feeling somehow that somewhere along the line there was someone in this stateroom who must have experienced great suffering. I have no way of knowing, of course. But perhaps you could talk to me sometime about it, and relieve my mind.

Yours sincerely,
Ellen Stewart

The last page slipped from his hand, and Vernon Grove sat rigid on the edge of his bed, listening to the faint far-off rising of the wind.

In the past few seconds it had begun to change. They must have left the Gulf Stream, or were on the edges of it. It was a current famous for its storms, a mysterious river of unnatural warmth, moving through the cold Atlantic, winding sinuously, changing climates, producing balmy weather in Bermuda, fog and rain in England.

He restrained the impulse to run immediately to Cabin B54, and cross-examine her. He picked the pages up and read them again, slowly this time.

He crumpled them in his hand, tossed them on the bureau, and then stood up and started brushing his hair rapidly. Seeing the look in his own eyes, he laid the brush down and smoothed the pages out, seeking certain passages, which he reread very carefully. A nineteen-year-old kid. From Sweet Briar College. Suddenly he tore the pages in half, and then into little bits. Moving to the porthole, wrenching it open, he tossed the fragments out into the dark windy night.

Maida Jennings had had golden hair, a honeyed skin, a beautiful body. Her mouth had been full, voluptuous. And her face could easily have been described as "not beautiful but . . . sensual," a face "eager and so avid for life."

Two years ago, aboard the S.S. *Columbia*, she had occupied Cabin B54.

Maida Jennings was dead.

The wind began to whistle past.

7

AMY HARRISON looked very attractive in black and white. She smelled expensive. Groomed to perfection, he lounged beside her in the gray light of the ship's theater, trying to enjoy this evening, hoping that the film he was about to see would divert him, distract him, restore his equilibrium.

Moviegoing in itself was one of his favorite forms of entertainment at sea, and practically his only contact with the outside world. There was no television in the mid-Atlantic. There were no newspapers for a week on end, and the ship's library was very poorly stocked. But the movies on the *Columbia* were changed every night, and many of them were shown long before they arrived on Broadway, first-run films from Hollywood, Great Britain, Italy and France, a conglomerate but always new selection. He had become not merely a fan, but an authority in the past eight years.

"Aren't these seats comfortable? Such a charming décor," Amy was saying. "Don't you adore going to the movies on shipboard? It's such a treat not to have to park the car, and stand in line, and smell the popcorn . . ."

He chuckled appreciatively. She was smoking a cigarette, smiling at him gaily. Her glances, her mannerisms were growing warmer every minute, her eyes softer, more languishing. Time has a way of telescoping on shipboard, and he knew that

Amy Harrison, in twenty-four hours, had fallen in love with him.

So, perhaps, had Ellen Stewart.

The lights went down. The newsreel began—the same newsreel which, though the feature would be changed daily, would be shown all week.

Ellen Stewart had simply written that morbid letter to attract him, excite him, draw attention to herself. She wanted to show off her uniqueness, her writing ability, her emotional sensitivity, and she had exaggerated an ordinary dream beyond its worth. As for the details, well, death dreams were common, and so were blondes. Funeral imagery was classic. It meant something Freudian. It was just his imagination and the coincidence of Cabin B54, which had placed far too much emphasis on the bandage, certain other phrases. These were random details, unimportant, and it was stupid to dwell on them. It was pure coincidence.

The feature was starting now. He settled back.

It had been made in Great Britain. He had never heard of it, and had never seen the star. But she was being talked about a great deal, a newcomer who had recently been discovered. He was anxious to see whether she lived up to her reputation.

The streets of London—Piccadilly, Whitehall—were passing before his eyes to an ultra-modern jazz accompaniment. And suddenly he was sitting bolt-up right in his seat, staring with his eyes transfixed.

This girl resembled Maida!

She was a blonde with a full voluptuous mouth, a face of sullen beauty. She wore her hair shoulder-length, loose and tousled, as Maida had worn hers. Her figure was about the same height, and its proportions—the full breasts, the slender hips, the very long legs—were very similar to Maida's. And the clothes she wore, the skimpy skirts, the off-beat styles, even her gestures and her way of moving, gracefully, erratically, were Maida's. They were stamped from the same mold.

Lowering his eyes from the screen, he gripped the arm of his seat.

But her voice pursued him. Coolly British, clipped, with its exquisite intonation, its refinement, even though the words that she was saying might be foul, it ran through him in the darkness with a silvery mockery.

"I will sleep with you, as long as it doesn't bore me, luv . . ."

Even her phrases. Even what she had called him. "Luv." Her special way of pronouncing it.

He closed his eyes. His toes curled in his shoes.

He had crushed her like a crumpled letter. He had torn her into bits and cast the tiny fragments far into the dark. He had cast her from him long ago . . . but now, on this windy evening, it was as though some ghastly jigsaw puzzle was beginning to re-form. The fragments were blowing together from nowhere, returning to destroy him.

Maida stood before him again, smiling her flamboyant smile. She swung her satin slipper at the bar and brandished her cigarette holder.

Maida Jennings had crossed on the *Columbia* from New York to Southampton in the month of October, 1964. He had first noticed her on the evening of the cocktail-mixer, the second night out . . . as this night was.

She was at the bar, the center of a group of men. Her dress was very short, of gold lamé, a glittering garment that outlined her body like the tail of a fish. Her tawny hair brushed her naked back, a back the color of honey. She was waving a jeweled cigarette holder, sipping gin and laughing drunkenly.

He hadn't gone near her.

He had watched her from across the room, tempted, but reluctant to begin the Game—at first. There was something about this girl, even then, which had held him back, something grasping and greedy, something dangerous, which had made him feel, even then, that to become involved with her would be a big mistake.

She danced with one man after another, and left—alone.

He didn't meet her until the following day.

October was a dull month for the *Columbia*, and there had been a dearth of pretty women on board. On the third day out he dropped into the lounge before lunch for a drink. She was again perched on a barstool, in tight green sweater and a pair of orange slacks, but this time only Harry was leering. All her escorts had deserted her. She looked bored and rather vulnerable. He slid in beside her, flashed his boyish grin.

"Good morning. I'm the ship's doctor. Welcome aboard. The name is Grove."

"Mine is Maida." The hazel eyes had glowed like stars.

Chatting and drinking with her that morning, he had found her far less brassy than he had at first imagined. She was British, with a voice that was a pleasure to listen to when she wasn't drunk, and she had a cool dry intelligence. Flippant and pert, swinging one slipper on the barstool, she made wicked little comments on the *Columbia's* crew and passengers—and the world in general—which had amused him greatly at the time.

"There is so much to howl about, luv. Today the only meaningful sound is a howl or a screech. The only meaningful act is a personal atrocity." She brandished the cigarette holder. "The slow sensual progress of self-immolation."

She was off-beat, irreverent, a rebel with a very light touch —on that gray October day. And yet she seemed to be so rich, patrician. She was descended from some obscure British noble family, she said. "The last in line. You've never heard of the beastly Jenningses? Well, you haven't missed a thing, Doctor." She laughed. But she went on bragging about her noble blood.

"We own a stately home in Wiltshire, luv. Glyn Tower. Ever been there? Oh, it's quite a museum piece." She had been born in India, spent her childhood there. "Father used to run the country, y'know." The huge emerald ring on her right hand had once belonged to a maharajah. "Of course it has a curse on it, darling, and do you know what it is? I'm single." She laughed, flirted with him, boasted, tossed the beautiful blond hair. She had a flat in London, but had also lived in Rome, Majorca, Acapulco, and Paris. "I suppose I'm one of those awful jet people. Do you loathe the type?"

She was "in the theater."

"In and out of it." She made a face. "I'm not much good, though I *try* bloody hard." She grew a touch more somber. "I've been in a couple of plays, walk-on parts, and had a screen test for Fellini once . . . but only Josephine has ever really believed in me."

It was then he learned that she was traveling with her private voice coach, a former actress, a Miss Josephine Ludlow. "She did things at Glyndebourne, and practically grew up in the music halls." They were sharing Cabin B54. "What a crummy little dive, luv! Josephine despises it." But throughout the voyage this woman was never introduced to him, and he saw her only at a distance. Dark and portly, middle-aged, she remained a shadow in the background, aloof, unsmiling.

. . .

"How are you enjoying it?" Amy was whispering to him in the dark, then smiling. "Were you asleep?"

"No. Just resting my eyes a minute. Do you like it?" he said.

"It's marvelous. She's terrific, isn't she?"

Her shoulder was brushing his, her hand was resting on the arm of his chair, and he knew that she expected him to take it, make some kind of intimate overture. So he lifted the warm fingers and held them for a minute or two. Then he released them. He could not sit still. He wanted only to get out of this place.

The wind was rising steadily. The velvet curtains on either side of the screen swayed back and forth. He could hear the engines far below, pounding and shuddering, as the ship braced herself to meet the impact of each stronger and fiercer wave. Even up here, in this gray cocoon, this unreal, artificial world of canned sound and canned faces, he could feel the ship beginning to swing in the great void of the deep, like a pendulum.

"I *love* you . . ." shrieked the voice from the sound track, rising above the crashes and the rattlings. "Don't ever leave me . . ." People were beginning to totter up the aisles, looking pale and sick. But Amy Harrison sat there, intent, enraptured. The face upon the screen grew huger and huger. It bore down upon him, in an enormous close-up. Tears as big as golf balls rolled down its cheeks. The golden hair was that of a giantess.

Sobbing and pleading, Maida Jennings looked into his eyes again, and crawled along the floor, disheveled . . . but this wasn't Maida, this was just an actress, an actress who had made this picture in some London studio with Kleig lights; and a booking agency in New York, with fat men smoking cigars, who didn't know him or Maida from Adam, had picked it out. It was all coincidence. He was reacting like a child.

The monstrosity ended at last, and the lights went on.

"Wasn't it wonderful? I was deeply moved," Amy said.

"Yes. Very good photography."

"I thought that scene where she went to the psychiatrist was so effective. And the man was good."

He hadn't even been aware that there was a man.

As they were passing up the aisle, somebody touched him. "Good evening, Dr. Grove," said someone with a low, hollow voice.

Spinning around, he saw that it was "Aunt Victoria." "Oh, good evening, Mrs. Graham." She was in black chiffon, spectral, haggard, grimacing and smirking behind her owlish spectacles.

"Did you enjoy the film? Did you find it *interesting?*" Touching him again almost playfully, she brushed past him with her twitching smile and hurried up the aisle without waiting for his answer.

"Who was *that?*" Amy asked.

"No one. Just a woman at my table."

"I've never *seen* her there at all . . ."

They stood together at the chilly exit. Her arms were bare, and she hugged them, shivering in the cold drafts sweeping through the ship. He knew that she expected him to conclude the evening with a drink, more dancing, and the inevitable proposition. At eight o'clock tonight he had had every intention of winding matters up that way. But he wasn't up to it. Right now. Not yet. Amy Harrison would have to wait.

So—"It's getting rougher," he said. "I'm afraid we're in for a real nor'easter. And my seasick cases are probably piling up."

"Of course," said Amy. "Well, it's been just delightful."

It had been just lousy. Ruined by that stupid letter. After he had escorted Amy back to her cabin, and shaken hands with her gravely at the door, he walked around the ship for a while, brooding, trying to rid himself of his deep feeling of depression. The spell the movie had cast still remained, and Aunt Victoria had put the finishing touches to it, but neither Mrs. Graham nor the film, he knew, would have so affected him if that crazy letter hadn't come.

Now, for no reason whatsoever, he didn't even want to go back to his cabin, enter those dark silent rooms which Maida once had shared. He was like a kid who had just read a ghost story. He kept seeing her, he kept remembering . . .

That afternoon in his examining room . . . that dreary afternoon in October . . .

"I have this ridiculous ache." In an abbreviated burlap shift she had hobbled in, across the polished linoleum. Eyes aglow, voice soft, she had perched upon his examining table, run her suntanned hand up and down one beautiful bare leg. "It *hurts*." Her body had challenged him. "What wonderful hands you have, Doctor. Strong but gentle. Do you think I sprained it, swimming in your pool?"

That was the first time he had touched her, yes, and he could remember the feeling now, the overpowering surge, the delirium. Even now, two years later, after all that had happened, he could still recall the melting smoothness of her skin, the look in her eyes. Walking about the *Columbia* like a drunken man, he could still lust for her—and fear her.

But she was dead, long dead. Buried in the antique churchyard of her ancestors.

8

ALL NIGHT long the gale blew steadily, the rain beat down upon the decks of the *Columbia,* and by morning the ocean was coursing past the hull like molten marble, licking at the bleak horizon. The ship was pitching and rolling violently. In heavy seas, life was hectic for the medical staff, and Vernon Grove was soon sucked back into action. He and his three nurses worked incessantly all night and well past the dawn. He came down to breakfast late and tired, very much in need of coffee and a hearty meal.

The Wedgwood Room was practically deserted, and showed all the customary signs of a rough day at sea. The chandeliers were lit, and curtains had been drawn over the portholes to spare the passengers the sight of the tilting, heaving sea. Although by now the stabilizers had been called into play, the rolling and shuddering of the ship were still pronounced, and small guard rails were set around the table rims to prevent the silverware and china from sliding off to the floor.

At his table, the only persons present were Father O'Connor and Aziz.

"Good morning, gentlemen—and congratulations." Smiling wanly, he slid into his place.

"Nothing could keep me from *these* breakfasts." The priest grinned, shoveling in a forkful of kippers.

"Iss beautiful!" Aziz giggled. "I *love*—like riding *camel!*"

His black eyes rolled behind their horn-rimmed spectacles. He seemed very full of himself. With an air of self-importance he planted both elbows on the table and leaned forward. "Iss somessing—exciting." He addressed Dr. Grove, and sat there grinning, waiting, until the waiter had taken the doctor's order.

"Yes?" Vernon Grove asked politely. "What's exciting?"

"We were just discussion," Aziz said. "I tell already the priest." He bobbed the turban. "Iss about Mees Stewart." He rolled his eyes toward her empty place. "Do you know somessing, Meestair Grove? She have ziss—ziss ability . . . Oh, *you* tell, Priest." He subsided with a giggle, waved a hand to O'Connor.

Vernon Grove frowned.

"According to Omar, young Miss Stewart is psychic," the priest said, smiling. "Or claims to be. She told Omar all about it up on deck last night. He got soaked to the skin, hearing about it. She apparently has the gift of ESP. Extrasensory perception." His eyes rested on Dr. Grove benignly.

Vernon Grove reached for the coffee pot. "Really?" he said. "Exactly what does she base these claims on, did she say?"

Aziz was distressed at the meager reaction. "She see ghos . . . spirit . . . past . . . future. PSC. She know what peoples *theenk . . . feel.* You no believe, Doctor?"

Vernon Grove forced a smile. "No, I'm afraid I don't, Mr. Aziz." The coffee in the pot was lukewarm, and bitter. He addressed the priest. "On the subject of ESP, I'm a born scoffer, Father."

"Hmph," Aziz sniffed.

The priest smiled at him tolerantly. "Really, Dr. Grove?

Well, I am not quite that sure. After all, psychic phenomena —and psychics are being taken rather seriously nowadays. For example, there is Dr. Rhine at Duke University . . ."

"Yess!" hissed Aziz triumphantly.

"And that Hollander," the priest went on. "Croiset, the one who has specialized in finding missing persons purely by his own unique psychic powers. I read an article on him recently, and I believe the police have even called him in on certain occasions to help them solve crimes. And he has actually solved them."

"Never heard of him," said Vernon Grove.

"You haven't?" The priest cleared his throat and stared at the brass chandelier swinging back and forth above their heads. "The brain, of course, is still an unknown country, in many respects—like outer space. And as a psychologist, I myself can believe that certain people, extraordinarily sensitive people, may possess special mental equipment which can tune in, as it were, certain waves, vibrations, even imagery, which other people cannot sense at all." He smiled. "As a priest, naturally, I cannot scoff at mystical experience. After all, the Church was founded on a miracle." He beamed upon his congregation of two.

"Yes, but . . ."

"Iss like Shakespeare," Aziz interrupted, nodding emphatically. "Iss many ssings in heavens and earth iss never dreamed of in your philosophy," he began misquoting reverently.

But the priest was turning the big bull neck in its clerical collar, and with a broad smile said, "Here she is. We'll ask her."

Ellen Stewart was making her way across the nearly empty dining room.

"Um . . . good *morning* . . ."

She wore a turquoise blue sweater and matching skirt. She looked as shy and demure and self-conscious as ever. Casting Dr. Grove a glance of bashful inquiry, faint reproach, she slid into her chair and looked around.

"Why . . . is . . . um . . . everything so dark?" she asked. "Why do they have the . . . um . . . um . . . windows covered?"

"They're afraid," Vernon Grove replied, "that the sight of the ocean might not be exactly conducive to eating breakfast."

"But it's . . . um . . . gorgeous today. It's so—*wild*. I wish we could watch it."

"Your aunt is still not feeling well?" Father O'Connor inquired as the waiter arrived.

"Yes . . . um . . . she feels much better, thank you, but she just didn't feel . . . um . . . like coming to breakfast."

Dr. Grove's breakfast was served, and then she floundered through her order, but the two men were obviously merely waiting to pounce. Aziz never took his eyes off her. The priest kept squirming in his chair. And there was no way of stopping either one of them.

"We were just discussing your, uh, what shall I call them, your psychic powers." O'Connor began the moment the waiter had departed. "Omar was telling us that you and he had a most interesting talk on the subject last night."

She looked at Aziz quickly, with a look of sharp annoyance, and then back at O'Connor, as if suspicious that he might be making fun of her. "Yes," she said at last. "We did."

"*Mos* inarresting," Aziz cooed. "Ver' *exciting*."

"It's not . . . um . . . something I'm *proud* of," she said, ignoring Aziz and looking at Dr. Grove. Her hand strayed nervously to her hair, and she fingered a strand. "It's a . . . um . . . *painful* to me."

"How so, Miss Stewart?" the priest prodded.

She paused before answering, then took a full breath as if making a determined effort to let the words flow without stumbling. "I *hate* to see terrible things. But I do. I can't help it. And it's a very bad thing to know what . . . um . . . people are feeling, even before they speak to you. To . . . um . . . read their hearts." She looked around the table with her great green eyes, at each face in turn. "I *hate* having ESP."

There was a heavy silence for a second or two. The brass chandeliers swung and the chinaware rattled and the sea roared past outside. Aziz and the priest exchanged glances, and then the priest said gently, "Just the same, Miss Stewart, as a psychologist I'm very interested in extrasensory perception. Could you tell us something about it, why you know you have it, how it happens, that sort of thing?"

She looked at him unhappily. She swallowed. "I . . . um . . . can't explain it," she answered in a low choked tone. "I . . . um . . . just know I have it. It's—I've had it my whole life. I've never . . . um . . . *wanted* to have it, or *tried* to have it, if that's what you mean, Father."

"I see. Of course. I understand, my dear. But could you tell us one instance, for example?" The persistent voice pressed on.

Vernon Grove stopped scooping up his scrambled eggs. "I don't think Miss Stewart likes discussing it . . ."

But the eager Aziz was already interrupting. "Tell room-mate. Mine disaster. Elevens peoples. What you tell to me!" He wriggled with excitement, spectacles agleam.

"Mine disaster?" asked the priest.

"Oh." Her cheeks were aflame. She twirled her fork. "That —that was just a *little* thing, Father. Nothing."

"Tell us." The priest was shoving his chair back and balancing his cup and saucer on his knee.

"All right," she said. "But it's just *nothing*. Really. One of the *lesser* things." Fixing her eyes on Dr. Grove, she spoke quickly, rather breathlessly. "Well, one night, when I was . . . um . . . about sixteen years old, in Marshall, Virginia . . ."

Down in Marshall, Virginia, she said, speaking with fair fluency now, she had awakened suddenly in the middle of the night, with a feeling of doom and darkness and a phrase ringing in her head.

"A voice seemed to be speaking to me, the words '*Eleven will die. Eleven will die.*' Over and over again. And I knew that it meant something. I knew, just as I knew before my roommate died, and my—my parents died, that something terrible was about to happen."

She paused, again as though trying to summon control, and the stabilizers crashed. The ship heeled, shuddered, righted itself.

"It was so strong a feeling," she went on in a faraway tone, "that I got up out of bed and wrote it down on a piece of paper. And then the next morning . . ."

"Yess?" breathed Aziz. His eyes were like brown marbles.

"The next morning, when my father brought the morning paper in from the mailbox, there were the headlines: *Eleven Die in Mine Shaft Disaster*. Those were the headlines." She paused, her face becoming sorrowful. "Eleven men had died, at the *very hour* that I had written the words down." She looked sadly at Dr. Grove.

"Well!" O'Connor said. "That's very, very remarkable. I

must make a note of it," he said. He placed his cup and saucer on the table and got up.

"It . . . um . . . um . . . maybe doesn't sound like much, but it is true."

"I believe you, child." He patted her shoulder. "And thank you. Coming, Omar?"

"Yess." Aziz, to the doctor's surprise, leaped up immediately.

"Did you . . . um . . . read my dream *ever*, Doctor?" she asked the moment they had gone.

9

FOR A SECOND or two he was tempted to lie. But instead, forcing a smile, he said yes, he had—though he was surprised to see that she had already discussed the matter with Mr. Aziz.

"Oh—but I haven't," she assured him, wide-eyed. "I didn't tell Omar a *thing* about it. Not what I . . . um . . . wrote *you*. I haven't told *anyone,* not even Aunt Victoria . . . about that dream. Just you."

"Why? Why me especially?" he asked casually.

"Because . . . um . . it seemed like something that only *you* could help me with. As a ship's *doctor*." Her eyes looked very earnest and innocent. "Was there ever anyone in that cabin like that . . . um . . . girl? Did anything bad . . . um . . . happen to her?"

Everything about her, at this moment, was so timid, so tremulous, so unsure. She was fingering a pearl button on her blue sweater. Her voice was faltering.

"Of course not." He grinned. "If there had been, I'd have been the first person to know it," he said. "That was just a dream, a nightmare, Ellen."

"No one . . . um . . . died there?"

"Certainly not."

"You *would* . . . um . . . tell me? You . . . um . . . *wouldn't* spare me?"

"Of course I would." He patted the slender hand. "Relax.

Forget it. That cabin isn't the *best* one on board, but it isn't haunted. Everybody who's ever stayed there has been extremely cheerful. And we've never had a single complaint."

"Really?" She still seemed unconvinced.

"Absolutely. Most of the people have been families. People with small children," he lied.

"In *that* . . . um . . . little room?"

"Oh yes," he said. "They put up cots. There's room enough. And I remember one couple from Philadelphia. Two alcoholics. They were in it last week. But the wife was a brunette. Yes, very dark. And they were always giving parties."

"I see," said Ellen Stewart thoughtfully. She had lowered her eyes at last. She sipped her tea. "But it's . . . um . . . still simply amazing."

"What's amazing?"

To prolong this discussion in this way, he knew, was dangerous. But at the same time he felt a compelling need to explore this young girl's mind, find out exactly what was there.

"The . . . um . . . *strength* of those vibrations," she replied. "From the . . . um . . . moment I walked into that cabin, Dr. Grove, I felt—oh, something very strange. A—a *presence*. An unhappy one."

"With your psychic antennae?" He smiled gaily.

"Yes. And all day, the first day, the entire ship depressed me. I couldn't . . . um . . . eat. I couldn't seem to—*leave* the cabin. I felt—oh, so m-miserable that I had come. A feeling of doom. A f-feeling of *death*."

"But it's all over with now, isn't it?"

"No." She shook the bright red head. "*She* is still there. There is still a *pressure*." She stared at the porthole, the curtained porthole beyond. "At times, I . . . um . . feel her *very* strongly, and then again, it's only the . . . um . . . *suggestion* of something trying to communicate. Like—like static on a far-off radio station." She smiled at him with wistful, sad green eyes.

The enormous room, with its waste of tablecloths, rocked and rattled. The sea struck the sides of the ship with pounding blows.

"But she has only m-materialized for me just once . . . in that horrible dream," she went on. "I have only seen her as she looked in that . . . um . . . coffin." Again she sipped her tea. "You're sure she wasn't in that cabin?" she asked again.

"Positive," he said. He slopped more coffee into his cup. "Don't take all this so seriously." He picked the cup up, moved with it over into Aziz's place. He summoned his most charming smile. "You're much too attractive a girl to take this stuff so seriously. I'd like to hear something about your life, Ellen. What was the name of that little town in Virginia?"

"Marshall," she said wistfully.

"Have you lived there long, Ellen?"

"Yes . . . my whole *life*."

She seemed perfectly willing to change the subject, eager to talk about Marshall. She loved Marshall, though it was just a very tiny village, she said, barely more than a post office and a couple of grocery stores, set in the foothills of the Blue Ridge Mountains.

Her face grew gradually more animated, her speech less hesitant, and she answered all his questions with a girlish ebullience he had never seen in her before. He even began to note certain small traces of a Virginia accent, certain Southern expressions in her soft, eager voice.

Her home was an old red brick house out in the country. It stood on the remains of an old plantation of two hundred acres. "It has belonged in my father's family for two hundred years."

"Was your father a farmer?"

"No." She smiled. "Daddy wasn't any *farmer*, I'm afraid." Her eyes grew tender and reminiscent. "The fields are mostly underbrush. But we still have the most beautiful of apple orchards, Doctor. Big . . . um . . . red apples, thousands upon thousands. Every fall the trees bear these perfect jewels of clustering fruit. And with no cultivation, no pruning, no spraying." Her eyes even grew merry. "My daddy always used to say the trees are haunted trees, and we must never pluck them, break the spell. The Little People take care of them, and the Little People deserve the crop."

"So the apples just rot away on the branches every year?" he asked her lightly. "That seems like quite a waste."

"Oh no." She shook her head and smiled. "The Little People come. They come down from the hills and pick them, and take them away." Her eyes grew bigger. "That's . . . um . . . true!" she declared, unsmiling. "By Hallowe'en, each year, they're . . . um . . . gone. Raked clean. And we have never had to . . . um . . . lift a finger."

He grinned at her for a second or two. Then he asked her pleasantly, "And have you ever *seen* these Little People picking the apples?"

"No. Well—*I* haven't. Though *Daddy* often did. Daddy had much greater psychic powers than I. Although once"— she dimpled—"once, in the autumn, when I was thirteen or fourteen, I was walking in the orchard at twilight. And I spied a very handsome man standing among the trees at a little distance. He saw me, and he smiled. He had coal-black hair. I had never seen him before. Then he . . . um . . . um . . . vanished, and I never saw him again." Her eyes grew dreamy and gazed beyond him. "My daddy always teased me about him . . ." She laughed softly.

Dr. Grove sat looking at her.

Everybody had left the dining room by now—except themselves, and the waiters. He had a batch of patients still to see, morning inspection to attend, but still he could not bring himself to leave this girl. She was a phenomenon, a fantasy. By no stretch of the imagination could he believe in what she was telling him, but on the other hand he could not call her a liar to her face.

"Your father sounds like an unusual man, Ellen."

"Oh, he *was*." She was all choked up suddenly. "A—a most unusual man." Looking up at her, he saw that her eyes were moist. "A poet and an artist—and a dear, *dear* person." She was trembling, on the brink of tears. "He died three months ago of a—of a . . . um . . . heart attack. And I miss him so. I can't—b-believe he's gone."

"I'm sorry."

The pale young face looked tragic, desolate. A tear was sliding down one cheek.

"You were the only child, Ellen?"

"Yes. And we had been together—alone—since my m-mother's death, when I was very small." Raising wet eyes, she seemed to be trying to control herself, and yet unable to stem the tide of memories, the need to blurt them out. "It was such a wonderful life, Doctor. A *solitary* life—but I loved it that way. I took care of him, and cooked for him, and we had a pet goose named Astarte, and he wrote beautiful poetry. And at night we'd sit before the fire, and read, or I would sing and play the dulcimer."

"The dulcimer?"

"That's an Appalachian instrument. It's very old. You hold

it on your knees and strum it with a turkey quill, and play the tune with a little stick we call a noter."

It was all such unusual stuff, she couldn't be making it up. It was unusual enough, and crazy enough, to be authentic.

"Did you ever hear the song 'Waillie, Waillie'?" she was asking shyly. "Daddy loved that best. Nobody knows who ever wrote the music for it, and he used to say that it was like music coming from an . . . um . . . an abyss of loneliness. The melancholy voice of a house."

"No, I'm not familiar with it," said Vernon Grove.

"He said it was like the . . . um . . . dust lying in old, old rooms. It reminded him of the . . . um . . . rustle of crinolines."

"Yes. Sounds fascinating," he said. He smiled quickly, and rose. "Well, I've got a lot of patients to see, Ellen."

"If I'd brought my dulcimer with me, I'd be happy to play it for you."

"Well, thanks. I'd love to hear it sometime. It was nice to talk to you." He grinned again.

"Oh, I have so much enjoyed it, Doctor." The green eyes sparkled. She was pink as a rose. "Thank you for listening. And you *will* think about that girl some more, the one in my cabin? You will, won't you?"

"Oh. *Sure,*" he said. "But—"

"I mean I haven't talked about her to anybody else," she said simply. "Not yet, Doctor . . ."

As he hastened across the room he could feel her eyes still following him—with their bright, intent, all-seeing gaze.

Marshall, indeed, existed. He looked it up in the ship's *Atlas.* It was a tiny speck, infinitesimal, in the Blue Ridge Mountains of Virginia.

10

E S P was something Dr. Grove had never given a second thought to, but all through that stormy day, as he moved about the stuffy confines of the *Columbia*, he thought about it a great deal; he debated the pros and cons. His entire instinct, as a doctor and a practical man, was to revolt against any aspect of the supernatural. And yet he also knew that extrasensory perception had its devotees and was being studied. Either Ellen Stewart from Marshall, Virginia, was deliberately and cruelly pulling his leg, or she was a supersensitive, sheltered being, out of touch with reality, totally at odds with her beatnik generation.

He kept trying to convince himself she was merely the latter. But the priest and Aziz had upset him too. The scene at breakfast before Ellen came in had seemed just too damnably pat for comfort.

Whatever Ellen was, however, he knew that he could not possibly escape her for the next four days. They were in mid-Atlantic. As the ship's doctor (and its only one) he was vulnerable, available to every phone call, any request, at any time of the day or night. She also happened to be his table-mate. He could only suffer her in silence, observe her with an eagle eye, be polite to her, and hope for the best.

The best, of course, at present, was that she was really clairvoyant. For if so, her psychic abilities must certainly be limited—to the vague and general. O'Connor and his "Hollander" to the contrary, it was rare for any psychic to "see" anything specific. She might, perhaps, by some wild stretch of the imagination, have sensed some sort of peculiar atmosphere in that room—and translated it into a nightmare. She might even have sensed his own aversion to Cabin B54. But beyond that, which in itself was extraordinary, she would, if utterly innocent, be restricted to indistinct impressions. It would be a test of her honesty if she went any further than she had.

Meanwhile, she *liked* him, obviously. That was something very encouraging, and important to maintain. Though she might set his teeth on edge, it was, in fact, imperative to be very nice to her, divert her, see that she was kept happy.

With this in mind, he went up to the cocktail lounge at six fifteen on that third evening and started looking around for her. The rain was still drizzling on the decks outside, and a warm, clammy sirocco had taken the place of the morning's gales. The cocktail lounge was jammed with people, noisy with the pent-up *joie de vivre* that always seized the passengers in bad weather. Almost everyone in First Class was there.

Bored and restless after yawning all day in their cabins, or huddling gloomily in deck chairs on the covered mezzanine deck, they had poured forth at eventide and were filling the huge gilt salon with the bravado and gaiety of people covering up bitter disappointment.

But Ellen wasn't visible.

Amy Harrison was. She fluttered her fingers at him, hopefully, from across the room, and smiled a bright invitation. Aziz was. He sat alone in a corner, sucking gloomily on a Coke, his dark eyes darting everywhere at once.

Harry was—leering at him, with the eyes of an old crocodile. "What's the matter with you, Doc? Lose something?"

"Go to hell."

Harry laughed and slapped the bar with his hand. "She's here," he said. "She's still got eyes for you. Since five thirty she was here. What's the matter with you, Doc? You slipping?"

Vernon Grove left the bar and wandered around the ship. At dinnertime he poked his head into the Wedgwood Room, but only Aziz and O'Connor and the Ewings were at his table. He loitered outside for a while, waiting for Ellen to show up. But she did not appear. Baffled, he took the elevator to the promenade deck, and here, in the lowering twilight, he paced restlessly up and down against the sticky wind.

He could call her cabin, but somehow he didn't want to talk to Aunt Victoria. He could walk down there and knock, but the thought of walking down that cul-de-sac, entering Cabin B54 again, repelled him unspeakably.

"What kind of sandwiches you got, bum?" Returning to the bar, he ordered another drink, and stood there in the silent room amidst the empty barstools.

"Tonight we got no sandwiches. I'll send the boy down for one. What kind of sandwich you like? What's on your mind, Doc?" Harry asked. "You not even eating in the dining room? What's that doll done to you?"

Harry's shallow eyes again rested just a fraction too long on him, and Vernon Grove felt his cheeks go hot.

"Nothing," he said. "It so happens I can take her or leave her alone."

"Yeah," Harry said. "I can tell that."

He ate the sandwich, and then idled in the lounge through the evening, sitting through the horse races, watching the doorway and the windows looking out on deck. He walked past her cabin door several times, and then went around and around and up and down the First Class deck areas. It was as though she had left the ship, completely disappeared. He realized that he hadn't seen her once since breakfast.

By midnight he gave up any idea of entertaining her and flattering her. It had been very stupid in the first place, and he knew that now. But still reluctant to return to his cabin, he prowled the upper deck aimlessly, tired, but still much too tense to sleep.

The wind was definitely dying. A gibbous moon was struggling through the clouds. As he stood beside the rail, staring moodily at the black horizon, he heard footsteps and saw a man and a woman approaching him.

It was Ellen—with Aziz.

"Dr. Grove!" She called out to him gaily. A shadowy sylph with flowing hair, she came toward him swiftly, in the fitful patterns made by the moon. "Isn't it . . . um . . . *marvelous* tonight?" she caroled, her eyes glowing from a pale silvery face. "Don't you *love* it up here? I do."

"Yes, it's turning into a beautiful night." He glanced at Aziz, who was standing in the background in stiff silence.

Abruptly she turned and addressed Aziz in smooth, silky tones. "Thank you for a nice evening, Omar. *Bon soir*, Omar. *Merci.*"

Aziz, for a few seconds, simply stood there as though appalled, then, drawing himself up haughtily, flashing his dark eyes, he muttered, *"Bon soir,* mademoiselle," followed by a few bitter words in Arabic, and stalked away.

"Really, Ellen. You shouldn't have done that."

For answer she merely moved closer to him, her coat sweeping free of her slender body, her hands gesturing toward the sea. "Have you . . . um . . . um . . . *ever* seen a more beautiful night?" Throwing back her head, she breathed deeply of the air, and then turned back to the rail. "It's so *wild!*" she exulted, looking up at the moon racing through the dark flying clouds, and below at the brutal ocean, still lifting and falling, still seething in the aftermath of the storm.

"What's *down* there, I wonder? What does it all *feel?*" she mused. Gazing down at the churning water, forming and destroying hissing patterns of foam, she spoke intensely, vibrantly. "If we could only know what it feels and it sees, how wise we all would be, wouldn't we, Doctor?"

"Yes, I suppose so, Ellen. You speak French to Mr. Aziz?" he asked.

"Yes. That's the only way we can communicate. He's much more articulate in French than English. And so am I." She smiled. "Did you have a good day, Doctor?"

"*Quite* good. Very busy. What did you do?" he asked.

In the moon's uncertain light she looked up at him quickly, and then gazed down at the ocean again. "A good day. Yes, Doctor. Quite a good day."

Everything about her tonight was so much more self-assured, even crisp. It was as though since breakfast she had added five years to her age.

"What did you do?" he asked again, uneasily.

"Oh—watched the wake a lot. I stood back at the stern and watched the path that we were cutting across the sea. It was like a highway. This evening it was as though the water was flowing back into the sunset, as though the road that we were cutting came from the sun, and as though we were moving onward in time, on into eternity."

Not over a single word did she freeze or gulp, or even hesitate. The phrases flowed with somehow a fine edge of mockery. And he knew that he should leave her, get away from this girl, but for some reason he couldn't. His feet felt glued to the deck, his hands frozen at the rail. "You're feeling more at home on the ship, I see," he remarked numbly. "And you're having fun?"

"Oh yes. Out *here!*" She smiled. "But I hate to go to bed, Doctor."

"Well, let's not," he said. "Would you like a Coke or something—in the lounge?"

She shook her head, then slid her arm through his. "I haven't been left alone down there for a single moment." She leaned against him subtly, and her voice grew throatier, more tremulous. "That woman is *still* there. That blond woman . . ." He could feel her shivering. Her long hair brushed his shoulder. "She is *still* communicating—strange new things."

"Oh—come *on*. Forget about it."

"I *mean* it." She crept closer. "I feel an—an un*remitting* horror in that room. I feel that she is trying to tell me something . . . something horrible."

Staring out into the darkness, trapped against the rail with her, he muttered, "Baloney."

"Did you ever hear of dead people entering the souls of other people?" she asked him in a shaking voice. "That's what I feel *she* is trying to do to me . . ."

"Oh, for God's sake! Stop it." And he had jerked loose from her—protocol forgotten. He was staring at her wrathfully, and she was looking shocked. "I'm sorry. Excuse me," he said quickly. "But honestly, Ellen—that's ridiculous."

"My daddy wouldn't have thought it was ridiculous," she said in a small, hurt, childlike tone. "He'd have helped me. He'd have searched the . . . um . . . whole wide world." She turned her back on him. The breeze blew her hair wide, like a great dark fan.

"Well, I'm sorry . . . but there's nothing in that cabin, I assure you, and it's simply childish on your part, Ellen, rather unattractive." He paused. "It's all in your own mind. It's psy‑ chological."

She turned around. The great eyes glowed. "Then you are giving up on me?" she asked him quietly. "For good?"

"What do you mean?"

"I shall have to start asking other people about her. Like the . . . um . . . stewards, and the other officers." She turned away. She drooped. "I don't want to. But my *daddy* wouldn't rest . . ." She turned the silvery face to him. "Do you want me to?" she asked him softly.

"No," he said. Half the ship knew about his romance with Maida, and would be happy to prove him a liar. He felt sick all over, suddenly.

"Why?" she asked.

"Because—because they'd only confirm my opinion," he managed to blurt out, "and they'd laugh at you, that's why!"

"You—wouldn't want them to laugh at me?" She was back again, close to him again, all breathless eagerness. "How . . . um . . . sweet. How kind."

What a devil. What an artful little bitch.

But he still could not get away from her. She had more up her sleeve.

"I have more information . . . other images." She was toss‑ ing her hair back and smiling up at him now, like an excited child. "All day today, new things and new impressions have been appearing, shimmering . . . the outline of her life, I imagine." She touched his wrist. "And perhaps if I . . . um . . .

told them to you now . . . Would snakes mean anything?" She looked up into his face, her eyes very bright.

"Snakes? For God's sake. Of course not."

"India?" She frowned, and turned her gaze to the horizon. "I keep seeing this snake, I think it is a cobra, coiled up in a wicker chair. And temples." She was speaking dreamily. "People bathing in a dirty river. That is India, isn't it?" She turned to him again. "Does that ring any kind of bell?"

"No . . ." he answered, hearing the hoarseness in his own voice now.

"Oh dear," she sighed. "Well, perhaps it doesn't *matter* . . . Doctor . . . though, at present, *India* is very strong. Was she English, could she have been English, by any chance?" she asked.

"Ellen, I'm telling you this woman never existed . . ."

But she wasn't listening. She was leaning over the rail, gazing down into the ocean as though it were a crystal ball.

"I see a castle," she said. "In the sunset this evening I saw a huge dark castle . . . with stone battlements. And a lonely road . . . a tiny car . . . and it was moving through a pair of huge iron gates . . ."

And there and then, on that lonely upper deck, in the windy darkness, Vernon Grove was tempted to commit murder. It would be so easy. It would be so quick. It would stop that soft, lying voice . . . in an instant, in a flash.

"What does it mean?" she was asking. "Do you know?" And the deck beneath him had become bottomless. The ocean was pounding in his ears, like a beating drum. She was turning, smiling at him sweetly with those great blank eyes.

"No. Of course not. It's crazy. Let's get out of here. Let's just stop talking about it." He seized her arm and dragged her from the rail.

And his voice, his actions were coming from the depths of a nightmare world, an abyss threatening to engulf him.

The rest was blurred, almost a total blank after that. He took her back to her cabin, managed to utter a few mechanical phrases, but what he said, or what she answered in reply, he could not remember later. He knew only that she didn't mention Maida again, use her name, or give him any further details. "Boy friend!" He recalled her saying only one thing, and in a tone of repugnance, in reply to some stupid question he had perhaps asked about Aziz. "Mr. Aziz is not my boy friend. I feel sorry for him. He's lonely." That was all he could recall her saying on the short walk down to Cabin B54.

And just outside the corridor, she had said something about his "future."

"What about it?" he had asked. "What do *you* know about my future?"

"Nothing . . ." Pale and windblown, she had smiled with just a touch of sadness. "I only know that in the . . . um . . . *past* you have been lucky . . ."

Taking his hand quickly, she raised it to her lips, and still looking deep into his eyes, she touched it delicately with the tip of her tongue.

"Good night, Vernon Grove," she whispered, and disappeared into Cabin B54.

11

FOR THE remainder of that night Vernon Grove lay frozen in his bed, which so often in the past had been the locus of orgiastic joy but which now was a torture chamber, and knew that he had deceived himself overlong. Everything was coming into grim focus now. Ellen Stewart was no innocent child from some hick village in Virginia. ESP was for the birds. She was a consummate actress who had been set upon him by the police, undoubtedly. He was in mortal danger, and a sitting duck, trapped on the *Columbia*, here in the mid-Atlantic.

"A castle . . . and a lonely road . . . a tiny car."

And yet time after time he brought himself up short, and in the manner of a man grabbing a beloved friend by the wrist, he cautioned himself to think clearly, not to panic, see it plain.

He reminded himself that no matter what Ellen told him, *she and nobody else could possibly know anything.* Nothing of any real importance. It was completely impossible, one chance in a million, that *anyone*, the police or anyone, could know, or even have surmised, what had happened on that October day and evening nearly two endless years ago.

He alone knew . . . and nobody else.

He had been lucky, incredibly lucky . . . just as that little bitch had said. But that wasn't the issue now.

Who could possibly know that he had even gone to see Maida on that cold gray drizzly afternoon?

Two years ago, at 2:00 P.M., the *Columbia* had docked routinely at Southampton, and routinely she was scheduled to sail right back to New York at midnight of that same day. Her owners never encouraged a longer layover in England, and for Vernon Grove, this policy had distinct advantages. "I'm sorry, dear. I wish I could get up to London [or Paris] for a day or two, but—we sail." This was his standard excuse for some occasional clinging vine.

He had used it on Maida.

She hadn't accepted it.

In his cabin, hanging on to the bitter end, she had flown into a tantrum and stormed like a fishwife. "But it's absolutely *stupid* of you, luv. Why can't you quit this bloody job?" In his arms, every night, she had been telling him how much he meant to her and how much she wanted to do for him. "We could live anyplace in the world, luv. You could *do* research. I'd build you a laboratory." Now, with the Channel Islands sliding by, she cursed him. "You're a stick, a cheat. I *hate* you!" She left his cabin, and slammed the door.

He didn't go up on deck to see her leave. He remained in his cabin, disgusted and sulking. When he heard the boat-train whistle blow, he was relieved to think that she and that glum companion of hers were finally on their way to London. Thank God and good riddance. Maida had been a big mistake, after all; his first impression had been correct: she had eaten him alive.

There had been nothing like her in his life before, no demands so incessant, so insatiable. She had consumed his total attention, from that afternoon in the examining room on. He had acted like a man in a daze, a man drugged, giving only lip service to his job, taking no notice of the other passengers, living only for those moments with her, in bed.

But by evening of that day, in his silent cabin, in the deserted bar, he was itching for her again, missing her golden flesh, her witchery, her quicksilver charm.

She had amused him, fascinated him, with her wit and her stories. Maida never for a moment had been dull. She had opened up a brilliant world to him, most of which quite possibly was false or exaggerated, but that was part of her attraction too. Had she been telling the truth about her family? Did she really own a castle in Wiltshire? And had that ring belonged to a maharajah? People on shipboard could tell other people the wildest tales, knowing full well their stories couldn't be checked, and Maida, very likely, had done the same, merely to enchant him. But it didn't matter. She'd been sensational.

Before midnight of that evening the ship developed generator trouble. All the westbound passengers were shooed away. The *Columbia*'s departure had to be postponed.

By morning, echoing only to the sounds of hammers tinkering with machinery, she lay at her dock, under a cold drizzling rain, and an irascible Anderson finally made the announcement. There would be an extra day's layover for those members of the crew who had no active duties to perform. Vernon Grove was one of the lucky ones.

Lucky, indeed.

He had paused only long enough to don civilian clothes, a raincoat, and a dark slouch hat. He found a bus leaving immediately for London. None of his shipmates were on that bus. They hadn't bolted from the ship as fast as he. He had sat alone in a rear seat, with a handful of nondescript English people, poor and shabby-looking, and no one had spoken to him, no one had given him a second glance all the way. In the crowded bus station in London, he had looked her name up in a phonebook, stepped into a booth.

"Come immejiately!"

She was home, alone.

She lived not far away from the bus station.

It was then nearly two o'clock of a rainy, foggy afternoon. The London streets were crowded. He couldn't flag down a taxi. Asking directions from one person, then another, he had eventually walked the distance to her street, but who would remember one more bewildered American tourist after two years' time?

Her flat was in Chelsea, one of a long row of shabby Victorian buildings, facing a misty square lined with dripping trees. He saw no one, and passed no one in that square. There was no doorman in her building, merely a set of name plates, buzzers, and a door that clicked open on a quiet hallway, a flight of stairs carpeted in red.

"Come in, luv." One of the doors on the second floor was ajar, and he heard her voice from inside, calling him breathlessly. And there she was, dressed in black satin pajamas, waving the cigarette holder, in a room of enormous size, a huge dim drawing room. A gas-log fire was burning, yellow curtains were drawn, and there were books, fine prints, pots of gardenias, her favorite flowers. Then she was in his arms. "I *knew* you'd come. I *willed* it," she whispered. He felt the wild delirium all over again. He felt ridiculously content.

For two hours (at least), they had remined on the yellow sofa, and the only sounds in the room had been their kisses and the hissing of the gas fire, the soft patter of the rain outside. Not once had the phone rung. Not a footfall or a voice had broken the deep silence of that building, its atmosphere of prim, hushed respectability. There had been no one in the tiny adjoining bedroom, no one in the kitchenette, the windowless bathroom; and the curtains had remained drawn. Not once had he been tempted to look out.

At four thirty or thereabouts she had fixed him a sandwich, plied him with Scotch. "And tonight there's going to be an opening. You can take me to the theater. Won't that be divine?" Sitting cross-legged on the floor at his feet, she had looked so radiant that he didn't have the heart to say anything, but when she leaped up to telephone the box office, he at last demurred.

"I'm sorry, but I have to be back on the ship by dawn, Maida, and I couldn't possibly get a train that late."

"What?" She stared.

"The last train leaves at nine this evening. And the last bus leaves even earlier. I'm sorry, but . . ."

"That's nonsense," she said.

"Now, baby . . ."

"You aren't going back to that stupid ship," she said in low, level tones. "You're staying *here* with *me*. Phone those idiots and tell them you are quitting. Right now, Vernon."

"Honey, that's unreasonable."

"It is *not*."

"It's impossible." Hauling his body from the sofa, he had offered her a smile. "They couldn't possibly get another doctor in time."

Scornfully she swept away into the bedroom, and slammed the door.

It was then just six. He heard the delicate chime of a clock from somewhere.

From the bedroom he heard silence. "Maida?" He rapped gently. "Come on out, baby, don't spoil everything. Let me take you out to dinner, maybe. I've still got three hours . . ."

No answer.

"The train doesn't leave till nine. I've never been to London . . ."

With a sigh, at last, he turned to his hat and raincoat, still tossed over a chair, and started hauling them on. He drained the last drop of Scotch from the decanter, munched on the last olive. "I'll see you in two weeks," he called. "I'll be back here in no time . . . and I'll call you from the ship, tonight," he promised. He heard nothing from that bedroom, not even tears, but just as he was making for the front door of the flat the bedroom door burst open.

She was dressed very elegantly, in the gold cocktail frock with a short beaver jacket over it, and she was pulling on a long white glove over the big green emerald.

"You've changed your mind about dinner?" he said.

"No. I'm driving you back to your ship," she said, with a very white, set face. "It's on my way."

"Your way? Southampton?"

"Yes. I've decided to go down to Glyn Tower tonight. It's *near* Southampton." Icily calm, evading his eyes, she brushed past him toward the phone. "I had a call from someone down there this morning that *lights* had been seen in it, so I was *planning* to go, if *you* hadn't arrived." She picked up the phone on the big antique desk. "It's no *trouble*." Her voice trembled. "I'd just *adore* to take you back to the *Columbia* . . ."

Her smile was brittle.

"Maida—look. It's raining . . ."

"Oh, don't be *silly*, luv. I'm a *superb* driver."

She had telephoned the garage.

And no one knew about that insane invitation . . . or even that he had finally accepted it.

No one . . . except perhaps the garage attendant and a truck driver . . .

But *they* had barely looked at him. They hadn't said a word about him in the past two years.

No one, except himself and Maida, knew that he had seen, or much less entered, her ancestral, isolated, museum piece, the rotting old dump known as Glyn Tower, on that rainy evening of October, 1964. His movements and her movements were known accurately only to two persons—Maida Jennings and himself.

And Maida Jennings was dead.

He must keep repeating that to himself.

Lying in his bunk, aboard the *Columbia*, in the dead of night, Vernon Grove kept telling himself that there was nothing, in the end, to fear.

The police were not clairvoyant.

There had been no eyewitnesses—except a dead woman and himself—to what had happened in that empty pile of stone hidden behind those high iron gates.

He must keep assuring himself of that.

No one knew a thing.

He must remain, as always, totally calm, totally collected.

The morning of the fourth day dawned, a peaceful, still Sunday morning. The horizon turned silvery, then pink, and soon the sun blazed out across the vast vacant green expanse, highlighting it into a sheet of diamonds. Vernon Grove lay in his air-conditioned cabin, watching the slow progress of the light, its glint upon the brass fittings of his porthole, its dancing warmth upon mahogany paneling and counterpane, its glitter on the silver frame which encased the smiling photograph of his son.

A discreet knock sounded on his waiting-room door. He froze. But it was only his room steward, Brooks, tiptoeing softly in.

"Oh, excuse me, Doctor. Sorry to disturb you. I thought you'd be at breakfast by this time."

"No . . ." He feigned a yawn, and stretched. "What time is it?"

"Nearly nine thirty, sir."

"Really?" He pushed back the sheet, then lay back. "Guess it's too late for breakfast. Would you mind bringing me some toast and coffee?"

"Certainly, sir."

With a pleasant, polite smile, the man departed.

Brooks was a West Indian, soft-spoken, ingratiating. He had only been on the *Columbia* a year. Lying back on his pillow in the dazzling glare, Dr. Grove was strongly tempted to question him, see what Brooks might innocently reveal, about the private goings-on in Cabin B54. Brooks, he knew, was a personal friend of Albert, Ellen Stewart's room steward. But by the time the man re-entered with his tray, he had changed his mind again. It might only lay him open, unnecessarily. The ship's grapevine was fantastically swift, the crew's quarters a rabbit warren. He could trust no one to be his friend. And if research was possible, it must be done in higher echelons—with care and caution.

"Going to be a hot one today." The steward moved to the thermostat, adjusted it, then stared out the porthole.

"Yes. Summer's back again."

"Lots of haze on the ocean. I wouldn't be surprised if we ran into fog by nightfall."

"Really? Oh, I think it will probably just burn off," said Dr. Grove.

He poured his coffee. He sipped it, ate his toast, slathering orange marmalade on it, staring at the ocean, wishing he could stay in this quiet oasis of a room forever, simply hide until Le Havre or Southampton. In the examining room he could hear the thud of chairs, the rattle of wastebaskets, the rubber wheels of his examining table being wheeled over linoleum . . . where Brooks was tidying up for the afternoon office hours. Even on Sundays he had office hours. There was no respite, nothing he could do except conform.

But his nerves were throbbing.

Soon the vacuum cleaner began to whine, a sound which he had always found irritating and today it was even more so. He fled into the bathroom, showered and shaved—and breakfast would be over by now, the purser's office would be open. Bob Jenkins was an honest man, and there were records, passports. The *Columbia* was a scrupulously run ship.

12

THE PURSER'S cubicle stood adjacent to the First Class dining room, and Bob Jenkins was alone in it, bent over a sheaf of papers, which he was marking with a yellow pencil. A thin, taut man in his fifties, a small mite of a man with wispy graying hair, the purser wore his habitual expression of harassment, but he looked up with a vague quick smile as Dr. Grove approached his counter.

"Morning, Vern. Things okay with you? How's the talent coming? Any names for me?"

"Not a thing at the moment, Bob. But I'll look around . . . Could you do me a favor?"

"Sure." The purser still pored over his lists. "You're a judge tonight, you know."

"Good God! Am I? Not again?" said Dr. Grove. He frowned.

"Couldn't do without you, Vern." Jenkins raised his watery eyes with a quick dry smile. "Your artistic judgment," he drawled. "As a matter of fact, there was some woman called up about you this morning. Wanted to know if *you* were in charge of this evening's clambake, and if so, she'd come." He chuckled.

"Who was she?"

"I don't know. Some lunatic." The purser waved his pencil,

stuck it behind his ear. "What was the favor?"

Vernon Grove took a deep breath. "I'd like to take a quick look at your passenger records. You know, the book, Jenkins. Names of a couple of patients of mine," he added briskly.

"Sure," the purser said. "Who are they?"

"I'll just look them up in the register myself. Just give me the lists, the book, okay?"

"We don't keep 'em in lists or in the book any more," Jenkins said. "New system. Since May. They're on cards. In a card file. But I'll pull 'em out for you. What names you want?"

For a second or two Vernon Grove hesitated. He looked toward the silent leather doors. "Ellen Stewart," he said. "And Victoria Graham."

"Stewart, Graham. Sure," said Jenkins.

And there was no particular change of expression on his face at all. Brisk and deadpan, just his usual abstracted self, he spun around in his blue uniform and started opening drawers, fiddling along the back shelves of his cubicle.

The information Dr. Grove was waiting for would have been copied direct from Ellen's passport, and her so-called aunt's passport, which they would have had to turn in for perusal at the beginning of the voyage. To see these records was the next best thing to seeing the actual passports of these women (which of course was quite impossible, unless he broke into their cabin). The purser, however, usually efficient, speedy as lightning, seemed to be taking an extraordinarily long time locating the cards. He fussed around. He scratched his head. He did a deep knee bend and disappeared behind the counter.

There was the heavy tread of approaching feet, and who

should loom into view at that very moment but Father O'Connor in his long black cassock, with a prayer book in his hand.

"Good morning, Doctor."

"Good morning, Father . . ."

The priest moved up to the counter ponderously and stood there at his side, beaming down at him. "How *are* you, my son? We missed you at breakfast. And at dinner, too, last night. And at luncheon—yesterday. Are you well? Is everything all right with you?"

"Yes. I've been very busy."

"Ah. You do look weary."

Meanwhile, the purser had abandoned his search temporarily and come forward with the ingratiating smile he reserved for First Class passengers.

"What can I do for you today, Father?"

"Nothing very much," O'Connor answered. "I'm in no hurry. I'll take my turn when Dr. Grove is finished." He turned his head and smiled unctuously—too unctuously, like a shark.

"Sorry to keep you, Vern." The purser returned to his shelves again, and then called over his shoulder, "Which Stewart was that again, Vern? Alice or Ellen?"

Dr. Grove felt his face flame. "Ellen," he muttered, hating the purser, loathing him.

For the priest was definitely relishing the scene—and relishing his discomfiture. The bland smile had broadened. The gray eyebrows had risen. And as Jenkins handed him the cards, there was a subtle sidling of the black cassock toward him. Not too obviously, but surely, the big bull neck in its white clerical collar was being craned.

The letters typed on Ellen's card blurred for a moment, but

then he read them, feeling his cheeks grow hotter and his spine grow cold.

They were exactly, perfectly, in order.

"Ellen R. Stewart, First Class," he read. "White, female, single, aged nineteen. Occupation, student."

And her address was Apple Valley, Marshall, Virginia.

Even the Zip Code was included.

And Mrs. Victoria Graham was listed as a white female citizen of the British Isles, city of birth Edinburgh, occupation none, and her age was seventy.

"Yes, Father, he's finished. What can I do for you?" he heard the purser saying.

"I'd like to send a cablegram—to England. Can I send it here?"

"No. I'm afraid you'll have to go up to the radio room. That's on the top deck, Father. Just take the elevator and turn right."

"Thank you, Mr. Jenkins."

"My pleasure, Father."

The priest strode off.

Jenkins grinned at him. "Got what you wanted, Vern?"

"Yes, Bob. Thanks."

Vernon Grove laid the cards down on the counter carefully, and walked away with an erect stiff stride.

Fidgeting away the remainder of that morning, moving through the farce of morning inspection, he grew more and more conscious of the breathless heat, the burning glare that shimmered from the ocean; aware of the silence that seemed to fill the corridors, so that footsteps coming toward him from a distance were more audible, laughter and voices heard from around corners or floating from the closed doors of cabins were peculiarly penetrating. He became acutely aware of the laboring thud of the old engines, the creeping pace of this wallowing white ship. He found himself standing amidships, or far up in the bow, unconsciously pushing, straining with his body, urging the ship onward, shoving it along faster.

His thoughts kept returning to the priest, to the scene with Jenkins, and the discussion of ESP the previous morning. He could tell himself that his suspicions had reached the point of paranoia—but *someone* had to be helping Ellen Stewart, and O'Connor looked and talked and even acted like a New York cop . . . in sheep's clothing. A cassock, a rosary, and a pious manner were pretty corny devices in this day and age. He had seen them in half a dozen movies. But there was also Aziz, the stooge, the foreign comedy relief, in his phony turban and his horn-rimmed spectacles. The two men seemed to be working hand-in-glove. Aziz, possibly, could even be from Scotland Yard—for the English police would certainly have to be involved. He probably spoke perfect English, was as hard as steel and wily as a cobra, one of those cultured colonials who had gone to Oxford, spoke at least eleven languages, and had been trained in Interpol, whatever that was.

It was lunchtime again, but he couldn't bring himself to face them. He felt suffocated, dizzy, nauseated. He ran down to his cabin, pulled his bathing trunks from a drawer, and took the elevator down to the swimming pool.

It was empty and echoing. They had just finished refilling it—after draining it during yesterday's storm. The salty water was very cold, fresh sea water, pumped direct from the Atlantic. He plunged in, and then, between the walls of turquoise tile, alternated between churning furiously, two and three laps at a time, and then floating face down, giving himself to the gently rocking ripples of the water as it rolled with the swells of the sea.

He had to know what was in that cablegram.

Dressed once more in his uniform, he took an elevator to the top deck.

Lounging into the radio room, he yawned elaborately, the most casual, the most nonchalant, the most bored officer on the S.S. *Columbia*. On the previous crossing he had treated the assistant radio operator for an infected finger, and while in the pool he had rehearsed an elaborate sequence of questions, but luckily, they weren't necessary.

"Hiya, Doc, what can I do for you?" The assistant was a young freckled Irish lad from New York.

"Hiya, Larry." On the desk, near the boy's right hand, was a correspondence tray containing a stack of carbon copies. "How's the finger?"

Larry held up the forefinger of his right hand, took a good look himself, and then showed it to Vernon Grove. "Fine," he said. "How's it look to you?"

Dr. Grove seated himself on a corner of the desk. He inspected the finger. "Cleared up nicely," he said. "Is that your dot-dash finger?"

Larry grinned, got up from his desk, stretched, and looked through the window. Dr. Grove's eyes darted to the tray.

"Good crossing?" Larry asked.

"I've seen a helluva lot better," Dr. Grove said. He stood— and couldn't move for a moment. "Lots of haze on the ocean —out there."

"Yeah," said Larry. "And hot as hellfire . . . Was there anything else in particular, Doctor?"

"No . . . just glad to see the finger's okay."

"Well, thanks. Thanks a lot, Doc," Larry said gratefully. "Thanks for dropping by."

It had been right on top. It was signed O'Connor. It was addressed to someone named Dawkins, with the code address of SUTQUAD, London. And the message had said: STUDY PROGRESSING WELL. END NEAR. MEET SHIP SOUTHAMPTON.

During his office hours that Sunday afternoon he received a phone call from the priest.

"He says it's vital," Miss Simmons said. "He insists on speaking to you personally."

"Vital? How?"

She shrugged and cast him a quick sharp glance. "He wouldn't tell me." She walked out and closed the door softly.

He sat back in his swivel chair, braced his foot against the desk, and picked up the receiver. "Yes, Father?"

"Is that you, Doctor?" brayed the nasal, overgenial voice. "It didn't sound like you for a minute. Sorry to disturb you, but I've been appointed as a delegate by the unholy six"—he chuckled—"to request your presence in the lounge tonight."

"The unholy six . . . ?"

Again the priest chortled. "Our table, sir. I keep forgetting we don't see much of you these days. But that's what we call ourselves. And we need your support. Can you make it, Doctor? Will you be there?"

"My—support?"

"Definitely. Ha, ha, ha. Some of us, believe it or not, have gotten up the nerve to enter the Talent Show," the priest bellowed merrily. "And we're hoping you'll come out and root for us."

"I see. Which ones?"

"We prefer to surprise you."

The priest hung up. He could not have sounded more genial, more friendly. But Dr. Grove's telephone receiver was slimy with sweat. His chair had made a gash in the mahogany paneling.

13

THE PLUMP soprano in purple was finishing her regurgitation of "Il Bacio" as Vernon Grove slid unobtrusively into a seat well toward the rear of the main lounge, ten minutes late for the ship's Talent Show. Pale but glittering, hollow-eyed but splendid, his fair-haired, brass-buttoned presence was noted almost immediately by two alert pairs of eyes: the purser's, who frowned at him and shook his head dolefully, as though in reprimand for being late; and O'Connor's, who grinned broadly and then raised a clenched fist up, down, and up again, as if he might be cheering on the Notre Dame football team.

He saw nothing of the others—neither Ellen, Aziz, the Ewings, nor Aunt Victoria. O'Connor was seated alone, up front, not far from the performing platform.

The huge salon was very crowded, stuffy, packed with people squeezed close together in rows on the uncomfortable folding chairs. It was jammed, as every Talent Show, crossing after crossing, was always jammed, simply because there wasn't anything better for the passengers to do on a dull Sunday night at sea. His eyes met the eyes of Amy Harrison, who was seated several rows ahead and had just turned round and was staring at him, with a quick smile and rising color in her cheeks.

Exquisitely dressed, she was raising her beautifully arched

eyebrows, cocking her pretty head—a painful reminder of time's distortion, time's forgotten hopes. Had it been only *two* evenings ago that he had danced with her in this very cocktail lounge, and only four days ago since he had stood beside her on deck, watching her wave goodbye to her husband? Time had no meaning any more, days had become aeons, and nights an eternity. Wincing inwardly, he threw her a grave smile, then turned his attention to the stage.

Two teen-agers in Beatle wigs were setting up a portable record player. And soon the music began twanging and jangling. The performers strummed imaginary guitars and formed words with their lips in synchronization with the nonsense syllables howling from the machine. "The only meaningful sound," Maida had said, "is a howl or a screech . . . the slow sensual progress of self-immolation."

The youths gyrated, hunched their shoulders, tossed their heads until the wigs swirled; wriggled, prowled, and strummed about the bandstand, opening and closing their mouths. The taller boy reminded him of the wolf in *Red Riding Hood*.

The crowd went wild. An encore was demanded.

Dr. Grove's eyes were on the huge grizzled head of the priest, the thick folds of the neck, the enormous shoulders clad so incongruously in their sacerdotal black. As the priest turned his head, following the gyrations of the performers, his profile looked coarse and brutal, the mouth cynical and hard. In the face of Thomas O'Connor in repose, there was nothing remotely spiritual or merciful. He had the tough, hard-bitten look of a man who would move very swiftly, and strike hard.

O'Connor was leaning forward now and snickering. Smoothing his enormous jowl with a huge hairy hand, he was grinning at the stage with smug enjoyment.

Stalking into view came none other than Omar Aziz, clad in his turban and a flowing robe, and carrying a black cardboard suitcase.

O'Connor turned around and caught the eye of Dr. Grove, as though enjoining him to see and enjoy. Once again he raised the clenched fist, a gesture possibly meant to signify "Fight on for Table 3."

Aziz opened the suitcase, set it up on a tripod, bowed, and flashed white teeth at the audience. "I do—the mageek treek." With a flourish he produced a deck of cards. "Peek card. Plizz. Anybody. I guess name."

Looking haughtier and far more sinister, the ungainly creature then began a staggering display of skill at sleight-of-hand. Bristling with self-importance, in the long robe pasted over with crescents and stars, he strutted majestically about the stage, shooting his cuffs in the manner of a professional magician, showering whole decks of cards between his long dark slender fingers. Abandoning card tricks, he started plucking quarters from the ears of the audience, silk scarves from breast pockets, all with lightning speed and dazzling effect.

O'Connor pivoted, caught Vernon Grove's eye again, and guffawed. "Yay, Omar!" he bellowed.

Aziz, burrowing in his suitcase, now produced and dangled aloft a pair of handcuffs. "I escape—thirty second. Put on— plizz."

A volunteer from the audience attached the handcuffs firmly to Aziz's wrist. "Iss real. Offeeshal. Like Houdini," Aziz hissed with a giggle. There was breathless silence. In a matter of seconds, seventeen by the purser's watch, Aziz had shucked them off, and there were loud cheers.

The band blasted prolonged fanfare, and Aziz smirked and

bobbed his turban, rolling his eyes about the audience, resting them, in glittering style, on Vernon Grove.

Yes. There was no doubt of Mr. Aziz's stupendous abilities.

But the band was segueing into "Charleston." And wriggling onstage to its gay beat, in a short fringed dress and a velvet headband, came Judy Ewing. Close behind her pranced the major in a straw boater and striped blazer. Table 3 was certainly well represented.

Shaking their shoulders and criss-crossing their hands and knees to the jazzy music, the middle-aged Ewings moved about the small platform violently enough to induce immediate heart attacks. The beefy major was very light on his feet, and very uninhibited for a sober retired member of the Armed Services. Mousy little Judy Ewing, who had seemed about as sexy as a prune, and had talked about the "natives" and international understanding, was now wiggling her hips, slapping her behind, and kicking up her silver heels with the abandon of a can-can girl.

Backing off, leaving stage center to his wife, the major extended an arm, and panted hoarsely, "I give you—Clara Bow!"

To the shade of Clara Bow, Judy did full justice. She danced, she twisted wildly, flashing black fringe and bright red garters. She even did the split at the end of her number. Then the major joined her for a mad finale. Purple-faced, they left the stage. But they were very good. They were much too good. They reminded him of old movies he had seen as a child, old musicals, with old-time vaudeville stars.

Vaudeville.

Maida had been "in the theater." She had had many friends, odd acquaintances backstage. Could his table have been packed completely? Or, worse still, could the Ewings have known her, known about *him*, and instigated this filthy, stinking game?

O'Connor was again turning around, smirking, winking, vigorously nodding his head.

And Ellen Stewart was walking out on the platform.

She wore a short simple white dress. The beautiful hair hung to her waist, satiny, burnished. An audible murmur of admiration rippled through the crowd. And he heard some woman saying behind him, "Oh, is *she* that lovely-looking little thing who never speaks to anyone? What's she going to do, recite?"

He couldn't imagine. He slumped a little lower in his chair and squirmed as Ellen stood there, speechless and pale, blinking the great green eyes and gulping.

"I am . . . um . . . going to play a song for you called 'Waillie, Waillie.' It is a piece I promised to play for someone on this ship. It was taught me by my . . . um . . . father."

He exhaled a quivering breath.

The purser hurried up with a chair, and she sat down and demurely smoothed her skirt. One of the band musicians handed her a guitar. "Um . . . *thank* you." She smiled timidly. Placing the instrument on her lap, she struck a chord, then cocked her head and frowned. The audience grew quiet. Her long hair slid across her cheek; she tossed it back, and again gazed shyly at the audience.

"This . . . um . . . piece should be played on a . . . um . . . different instrument. The dulcimer, but I haven't one . . . um . . . here, and . . ." She struck a few more chords. "It is the story of a girl whose love was rejected, who was left by her lover, and—" She broke off. She tossed her hair, and tilted her head back, and began to sing.

Her singing was faultless. Her voice, untrained but true, was the purest of sopranos, light but plaintive, filled with melancholy. Over the crowd it floated, and every word she sang was clear, full of a strange, poetic beauty.

> "When cockleshells
> Turn silver bells
>   Then shall my love return to me.
> When roses blow
> In winter snow
>   Then shall my love return to me . . ."

He kept trying not to be impressed, or thrilled. The meaning and the purpose were so obvious. He was being deliberately softened up, brainwashed by this crew of sadists. And yet, listening to that soaring soprano, gazing at her rapt face, he could not quell the illusion that the song was beautiful and *she* was just a simple artless girl.

> "Oh, Waillie, Waillie,
> But love is bonny,
>   A little while when it is new . . ."

This haunting minor music cast a spell. And so enchanting was it that he could, in these few minutes, dare to imagine, hope to envision her as singing it before the fire of an old plantation house—with apple orchards outside and a pet goose named Astarte at her feet.

> "But it grows old
> And waxeth cold
>   And fades away, like evening dew . . ."

The last strain died away, and she sat there quietly in the simple white dress, with her bright head bowed. The audience remained silent. Ellen rose and started walking off. There was then a long ripple of applause, and once again silence, as if the audience were still under the spell of her voice and her song, her spectacular appearance.

"Gave me goose pimples," he heard a woman whisper. "Who is she, anyway?"

And then he heard himself starting to clap loudly. He clapped and clapped as rising pandemonium ensued.

He felt a hand tap him on the shoulder. "Ready for the judging now, Vern?" The purser was smirking down at him, his eyes cold blue.

"Well, that's quite a table you've got there, Vern," Jenkins was saying. "What do you do, rehearse 'em in your spare time?"

"I didn't know they were even talented," murmured Vernon Grove. "This is all news to me."

He and the purser and the chief engineer, who was the third judge, had retired to a corner of the main lounge, where their deliberations were being watched nervously by the audience.

"Well, I vote for the redhead," the chief engineer said. "She was crazy, man, better than Joan Baez."

"I didn't think the soprano in purple was too bad," Dr. Grove mumbled.

"The *soprano?* Are you out of your mind, Vern? I agree with Hendricks," Jenkins said. "Miss Stewart was the best. Which makes it unanimous."

"What do you mean, unanimous?" Dr. Grove asked. "How about me?"

"Aw, *Vern.* Come on. Who you trying to kid, boy?" Jenkins elbowed the engineer in the ribs. "I've seen the way she's been looking at you. Wasn't that you and her up on deck last night?"

So the decision was unanimous. Aziz was voted second best, and the Ewings third.

Jenkins picked up three packages and mounted the stage. The audience quieted down and hummed with expectancy.

"Ladies and gentlemen," he bawled, "after long and due consideration"—he was interrupted, as he always was, by laughter—"the judges have reached their decision. Third prize goes to that pair of razz-ma-tazz Charleston dancers, Major and Mrs. Ewing from Fort Lauderdale, Florida!"

In character, these two veteran troupers slid across the stage, doing Charleston steps, bowed in unison to the applause, accepted their prize, and danced back to their places.

"Second prize," Jenkins announced, "goes to the young man who thrilled us all with his magic tricks. Mr. Aziz—from Basra."

Strutting forward in his robe, Aziz took his package, tried to shake hands with Jenkins, got his hands criss-crossed, and with a particularly piercing giggle left the stage.

"And now, ladies and gentlemen—our first-prize winner. A little lady, a very talented little lady—from Dixie. But I'm not gonna present her award myself. It is perhaps more appropriate that this award should be presented by one of my compatriots, particularly appropriate considering everything. Ah, will, ah—will our good ship's doctor, Dr. Grove, kindly step forward and make the presentation?"

Vernon Grove cursed. But every eye was turned on him now, and he could do nothing else but rise and walk grimly forward. "Vern . . ." Jenkins handed him the package. "Bastard!" he muttered close to the purser's ear, then he turned and smiled at the audience. Behind him, he heard Jenkins cackle.

"Ladies and gentlemen," he said, looking out over the rows

of heads, "it gives me very great pleasure to present first prize to Miss Ellen Stewart. Will Miss Stewart please step forward?"

Blushing radiantly, she rose and came shyly forward as the applause broke out. *"Thank* you," she whispered breathlessly, with green eyes shining.

"Congratulations, Miss Stewart." He handed her the package. The applause was coming now in waves.

"What's in it?" she whispered, leaning toward him gaily.

"Perfume, I imagine . . ."

"Gardenia? Oh, I hope so. That's my favorite . . ."

She slid her arm through his, and the audience was going wild. There were whoops of delighted laughter now. She started walking with him off the stage, speaking in a low voice to him, rapidly.

"Where have you been? I have seen more things. I have new images for you. White gloves. Does that mean anything? And candles. Three candles burning. I have seen the inside of that castle. There's a staircase, suits of armor . . . and two people. There's a man with her. They're going up the staircase."

He broke away. The crowd was getting up and people were bearing down on her. He left her to their mercy and started elbowing his way frantically toward the doors. He could not seem to breathe. His heart was burning in his chest. White gloves. A staircase. *Three* candles. Who? And *how?*

"Dr. Grove! For heaven's sake, you aren't *leaving?"* a shrill feminine voice piped, and his sleeve was caught. Judy Ewing's arm slid through his own and squeezed it tight. "Come on and celebrate. *Daddy's* paying."

"I'm sorry, Mrs. Ewing. No, I can't, Mrs. Ewing."

"Oh, come *on.* One little drinkie. Ellen will be so disappointed."

"I'm terribly sorry. Thanks, but—" He was panting, struggling to jerk his arm free.

"You can't even spare a minute for us, Doctor?" She let his arm go. "Oh, that poor child!"

"What's so poor about her?"

"Why, don't you realize," she asked, cocking her sharp, birdlike face, "you have that poor little thing so in love with you she doesn't know what to do?"

Then she went flouncing off.

He bolted for the exit.

14

WHITE GLOVES. Three candles. And a staircase . . .

Who?

And *how?*

On the night of October 18, 1964, the most regrettable night of his life, Vernon Grove had encountered only three human beings. One was Maida, one was a garage attendant, and the third a truck driver.

The garage attendant had brought Maida's car around to the flat in the pouring rain. And to him, Vernon Grove could have been little more than a silhouette, a tall shadow standing in the dimly lit doorway of that Chelsea vestibule.

The night was not merely rainy, it was foggy, very raw. Beyond the sleek wet sidewalk, the small low-slung car pulled up to the curb. The attendant climbed out, and Maida met him. She took the keys, tipped him, and slid in behind the wheel. Vernon Grove heard the only words she said, and they were "Thank you so much, Ferdie. 'Night."

The attendant hurried off, whistling, hands in his pockets, cap down against the rain.

Not until then did Vernon Grove descend the stoop and cross the sidewalk to the car.

His hat was pulled down low, his coat collar turned up, and to his best recollection, there had still been no one on that quiet street, no one visible in that misty square. Silently and quickly he slid into the car next to Maida, slammed the door shut, and they started off.

Those had been the only seconds when he could possibly have been seen two years ago—by the garage attendant or by someone peering out a window. But no one, in the past two years, had ever come forward and reported him. In fact, the garage attendant had stated, two years ago, that Miss Jennings, to his best knowledge, had been alone in the car.

The solemn muffled clangor of Big Ben was sounding the hour of seven as the car pulled out of the foggy square. Then it picked up speed and soon was whizzing past the lights of London, jerking short at stoplights, fighting traffic, one among a thousand cars jostling for position in the rain.

"You can still drop me off at Victoria Station, or the bus depot."

She shook her head, and he slumped lower in the bucket seat. The small car, a foreign convertible, had very little head or leg room, enshrouding side curtains, and he would have had to be practically invisible to any passer-by.

She was an excellent driver. But her hands in their white gloves were incessantly on the horn, or fiercely twisting the wheel with angry impatience. She took chances like a New York cabdriver, bullying her way through and jamming on the brakes. She managed her car as she would have liked to manage *him*—if given half a chance.

Once they reached open country, he began to feel drowsy. Resigned, relaxed by the Scotch and the afternoon's love-making, he fell asleep. When he awoke, they were jolting over cobblestones, through a village of low houses with thatched roofs.

"Where the hell are we?" he asked her sharply, peering around.

"Near Southampton."

He didn't recognize the environs, and there was no glow in the pitch-black sky that might indicate a city. He could see only open fields, low hedgerows, and stretches of woods, all faintly visible in the headlights. The road had narrowed. It was full of curves.

"You're taking a back way there?" he asked.

"No. We're stopping off at Glyn Tower first." She pressed down hard on the gas pedal. The car skidded crazily around a curve.

"I want you to see the place," she said. "It belongs to me. It might improve your *education*, luv." With the glimmer of a smile she turned the wheel suddenly, and without slowing down they left the macadam road and plunged into a side road that was little more than a lane. It was full of ruts. Tree branches clattered over the canvas top, thick woods surrounded them, and still she drove the car as though it were a horse that she was whipping to win a race.

"Look, Maida . . . no kidding . . ."

"Here we are," she said.

Huge iron gates loomed from the darkness. Stately trees formed an aisle beyond. It was so unexpected a spectacle after all those dripping woods, out there in that forlorn, forsaken countryside, that he sat bolt upright, definitely uneasy. No lights were visible, no house, as slowing down the car she entered the long driveway.

It was as though they were moving through the lonely precincts of a cemetery. There was the same unearthly stillness everywhere. The landscaping, the lawns that he could glimpse through the mist on either side, the shrubs, the trees which seemed to be clipped into fantastic shapes, looked manicured, unreal, and artificial—like a cemetery.

Maida began to talk about it, boast about it, as the wheels crunched steadily over gravel.

"In the summer there are peacocks on these lawns. Perhaps a dozen. And a flock of sheep. Did you know that sheep save money on gardeners? They keep the grass cut. You can also eat them, and get money for the wool." She smiled. "Oh, it's really quite an empire, luv, a feudal paradise. But not entirely a white elephant. You see, after Father died, Mother started showing it to tourists. To save on the death taxes, y'know . . . and those silly Americans have been a *boon. Cartloads* of buses every week, photographs and picture postcards, you'd be surprised how much it amounts to in a year. So I've let them come, since it doesn't bother *me*, jolly not. I have my flat, and my *career*." She laughed. "But it's all shut up for the season now. The caretaker and all those funny little hostesses are gone."

On she rattled.

"Sometimes, of course, I open it—for a fortnight, or a weekend house party. For the quail. Or fox hunting. And *that's* rather fun. Though it's terribly hard, of course, to get the proper servants in this mucky place. I usually bring along a caterer . . . Well, there's dear old Glyn Tower." She stopped the car. "What do you think of it?"

He caught a glimpse of a pond and statuary. He peered through the windshield glumly at stone walls and battlements streaming with rain.

Maida said, "It goes back to the fifteenth century."

"Great," he said.

"Christopher Wren did the eighteenth-century wing, and Adams did the ballroom ceilings."

"Interesting."

"There's a bedroom that Queen Elizabeth slept in." She

turned the motor off. "Come on, I'll show you." And she was out of the car immediately, running through the rain.

"Maida—I don't have much time."

She was standing before a huge wooden door, thrusting a key into a huge iron lock.

"I'll see it *next* time," he said.

Massive hinges creaked. The smell of old stone floors and cavernous darkness, furniture polish, and the faint rancid smell of things decaying, things unused, assailed his nostrils. Something squeaked and scuttled over the floor beyond, but she laughed and stepped inside.

"Come in! I'll give you the entire tour. For nothing!" Her voice rang out, and echoed. Her footsteps clicked over stone. "What the hell is the matter with these bloody lights?" he heard her mutter querulously, and then the striking of a match. A candle flared. She turned, her face a floating mask in the dark, and she was holding a candelabrum, a large three-branched silver candelabrum, with three white candles burning. Their light illumined a table of oak and a room crammed full of objects, like a museum.

"Shut the door, luv, or you'll blow the candles out," she ordered, smiling.

She had dragged him on a tour of the vast deserted monstrosity, insistent upon describing portraits, porcelains, suits of armor, sets of silverware. Holding her candelabrum aloft, and mimicking the manner and the voice of a tourist guide, she wasted his time, deliberately, with dates and anecdotes and silly references. It was all done mockingly, for Maida, too often in his presence, had expressed disgust, even hatred for the British Establishment.

"*This* one of my ancestors brought over from France—after

we beat Napoleon. And *this* is my father's collection of Indian ivories. This was my great-great-grandmother done by Gainsborough. And *this*, my love, was worn, actually used in the Battle of Agincourt, when we defeated the French. See the blood?" She drew the sword from its scabbard, thrust it under his nose. "That's blood, Vernon, *French* blood, fifteenth century, still there on the steel. Isn't that *exciting?*"

"Yes." He nodded, hating her.

Glancing at his watch in the so-called Adams room, he saw that it was midnight.

"And it will all be yours, Vernon," she was saying.

Touching the strings of some invisible harp that twanged and jangled on his nerves from the deep shadows, she waited, then came smiling toward him, behind her guttering candles. "It *could* be, you know." She came close to him, so close that he could feel the heat of the candle flames on his face. "Did you ever *see* anything like this—in Brooklyn? Or the entire *world?*" Her voice had a strange tremolo, and he moved toward the door.

"I've got to go, Maida."

"*Don't* worry about your silly ship. I'll get you there. It's only a few miles from here." Again, all agog, her hair a golden aureole, she was brushing past him, holding her candles high and running toward a wide wooden staircase. "You haven't even seen Queen Elizabeth's room. The Red Room. That's the coolest."

He could see her legs, her shimmering silken legs, and her very short metallic skirt flashing up the stair treads. She paused, looked down at him, and for an instant her eyes melted. There was that aching, naked look in them he knew.

"Come *on*, luv," she whispered softly.

He trudged slowly up that staircase behind her, yes, God help him, thinking that he still had a few hours to spare—and the three candles danced ahead. Their shadows loomed large on the walls.

Vast and chilly—and sepulchral—had been the Red Room —something out of Queen Elizabeth's day. The canopied bed resembled a catafalque—and the combination of the rain out side, the huge gilt mirror opposite, and the presence of some very huge, oppressive wardrobes near the door were scarcely conducive to desire, even the pretense of it. The bed was lumpy, the crimson coverlet dusty. "What's wrong?" she asked in a cold stiff voice, lying rigid in his arms at last. "Don't you love me any more?"

"Of course I do."

"Then what is wrong?"

"Nothing."

"You are thinking of your ship—and your mucky *harem!*"

"Don't be ridiculous." The rain beat down steadily. He lay there listening to the wind and rain, feeling the coldness.

"You don't like my house?" she asked.

"Sure. It's—terrific."

"You *hate* Glyn Tower." She laughed. "You think it's ghastly and evil—and it *is*, luv. Full of evil. Full of wickedness. Full of wars and cruelty and lust . . . Did you know that there are dungeons underneath this place? I didn't show you the dungeons, did I?" She lay there laughing softly, and he tried to rise, but she caught his arm. "My ancestors were an evil lot, luv." She lay across the bed, sprawled there, half naked, stroking his arm. "But you're an American, my sweet, —*so* pure—and so naïve."

"What does being an American have to do with it?"

"Fresh blood." She laughed, and twined her arms around

his neck, trying to draw him back down, trying to kiss him. "Aren't you a snob, darling boy?"

"Come on, Maida. It's late."

"You don't *like* luxury? Just a teeny-weeny little bit?" She kissed him, then she bit his ear, really bit it, and it hurt like hell.

"For God's sake . . . cut it out!"

"Beautiful meals," she said, giggling, "served on beautiful silverware? You wouldn't want to be a grand seigneur? We could live here, you know, ride to hounds, give balls. You could run for Parliament, be knighted, wouldn't that be fun? Sir—Vernon Grove—Baronet?"

He untwined those clinging arms. He struggled out of bed. "Let's be serious," he said. "Are you going to drive me to the ship now, or do you want me to hitchhike?"

There was ominous silence. He began to dress. Groping for his tie along the icy floor, he heard her sobbing.

"I'm very sorry . . ."

In the huge dim mirror, lit only by the light of the rain outside, he could see her rising from the bed, a disheveled shadow.

"I'd be *good* to your son!" She grabbed him from behind— a harridan. She sobbed against his shoulder, slobbering wet tears. "I'd give him a pony—and a tutor—and this *house*, Vernon. Oh, Vernon, love, my love, don't leave me, please. Don't you realize how I want you, how I need you? I'll be alone . . . *alone!*" Her voice rang out theatrically.

"Come on, Maida, let's go."

He started toward the door, with her body dragging on him, her hands clawing him. "I'll kill myself! You'll be sorry . . . *Wait!*" she screamed. And the echoes shrilled from the dark walls. "*I'll* drive you back! *I'll go* with you!"

"Make up your mind then, for God's sake!"

He turned. The tears were streaming down her cheeks in the shadows, her hair tangled on her naked shoulders. But he also saw a gleam in her eyes.

"But only on one condition," drawled her voice, "that you tell your captain you are leaving the ship. You are quitting, and staying here with me."

"I can't. You know damned well I can't."

"All right, I'll go aboard with you, and *stay* with you . . ." Calm and tearless was her voice, almost lilting. She started stroking his arm, squeezing and pinching it. "And if you try to stop me, I shall tell the captain what you are, and what you do—and then he'll throw you off that ship, won't he, Vernon?" She laughed. "Blackmail? Possession? You don't like to be possessed?" She gazed up brightly, and her eyes were demented. Her fingers moved up his sleeve, plucking at his arm, and it was a touch that made his flesh crawl. "It doesn't matter to me. You will learn to like it, luv. You won't get away from Maida Jennings so easily . . ."

"Will you cut that out, God damn it!"

He gave her a shove. She screamed, and bit him. He wheeled and struck at her, blindly, in the dark.

15

ABOARD THE S.S. COLUMBIA, *July 13th, 1966*

8:00–9:30 A.M. Breakfast, Wedgwood Room
10:30 A.M. Conga Lessons, Main Lounge. Ping-pong
   semifinals
11:00 A.M. Bouillon Served on Deck

Attention Everyone: Don't forget Gala Masquerade Party, starting 9:00 P.M. tonight, Main Lounge. Start preparing now. Exercise your ingenuity. Valuable prizes given for best costumes. Check your steward for suggestions.

PHILIP DOYLE had been aboard the S.S. *Columbia* for ten years, which made his tenure two years longer than Vernon Grove's. A dark, heavyset man, with shiny black hair parted in the middle and bold protruding eyes, he was now in his early forties, he had a wife and four children ashore, and it was he with whom Dr. Grove's nurse, Nora Murphy, had been carrying on an affair for the past three months. Doyle's rank as dining-room steward was far beneath Vernon Grove's on the *Columbia*, but between the two men there had grown up a kind of specious, bantering relationship. They had one thing in common, the Game, though Doyle was known as the Plunger, backstairs, and his tastes, in general, were coarser than Vernon Grove's. Their relationship was typical of most relationships aboard the ship. Nobody really liked or admired anybody else, but they were friendly, very friendly, all buddies, all lost souls. In any such listing, of course, Anderson, the chief exec, was excepted, and here the order was reversed. Nobody was friendly with Mr. Anderson and he was friendly with nobody, but he was admired, respected—and feared.

Doyle's door was ajar. "Phil?" Vernon Grove said, and pushed it open.

Doyle was personally responsible for the seating arrangements in the Wedgewood Room, and possessed his own private information on the passengers.

"Who is it? Oh, come on in, Doc. How's the Doc?"

Doyle, visible through the bathroom doorway, was standing before the washstand, clad in undershorts. His face was covered with lather. "What's up, Doc?" he asked cheerily. He continued to shave.

Vernon Grove sank down on the unmade bunk, his eyes darting around the small cluttered cabin. "I'm looking for a copy of *Time* magazine," he said. "For April sixteenth. You happen to have it?"

"*Time* magazine?" Doyle turned from the mirror. "Man, you know I don't go in for that high-class stuff." He dipped his razor with a grin. "That's the most flattering thing you've ever said to me."

Vernon Grove smiled wanly.

"You tried the library?"

"Yeah, they don't have it."

Doyle was regarding him in the washstand mirror now, with his protruding eyes. "You don't look so good today, Doc. What's the matter? Off your feed or something?"

"No, just overworked. That stinking Brightwood . . ."

"Yeah, that was some dirty trick to play on you," Doyle

said. "I'd have him kicked out of the medical profession." He set down his razor and started clapping water to his face, blowing and snorting, and then patted his jowls with a towel.

Vernon Grove stretched out on the bunk. The cabin was very hot, well below decks, and close to the engine room, and the clanks and thumps of the machinery were very audible. But he wished that he could stay in this cluttered, airless little hole and simply sleep all day.

Doyle emerged, hairy and vigorous, and stood grinning down at him. "But buck up, Doc. The trip is almost over with. They'll get you a new boy in England, you'll be swinging like you always have."

"Do you think so, Phil?"

"Do I *think* so?" Doyle's laugh rang out heartily. "You're one guy who's got the greatest powers of comeback that I've ever seen on anybody, man." He reached into a bureau drawer and pulled out a clean white shirt. "Yeah. You'll recover." He started unbuttoning the shirt, still chuckling.

"I want to ask you a personal question, Phil."

"Sure," said Doyle, smiling.

"Do you think I'm slipping? They're trying to ease me out of here?" Hands behind his head, Vernon Grove stared at the ceiling.

"Slipping? Whaddya mean? What the hell are you talking about?" Doyle cried.

"Oh, it's just a feeling, Phil. Nothing in particular. Except —well, there's my table, for instance. You used to give me a few V.I.P.'s, at least a bank president or a factory owner, and that's the damnedest bunch of bananas you've ever handed me."

Doyle started hauling on his shirt, in silence. Then he said rather stiffly, "What's wrong with them?"

"Not a V.I.P. in the carload," Vernon Grove said. "Duds. Jerks."

"We didn't get many V.I.P.'s this trip," Doyle said. His tone was aggrieved. "We got exactly *three*, Doc—the assistant manager of the Cleveland Symphony, some attaché from the Brazilian Embassy, and we got a twenty-eight-year-old disc jockey from Louisville." He ticked them off on his thick fingers. "I had to put 'em all at the captain's table. Hell, what's wrong with *your* people? Haven't you got the redhead? What's so wrong with her?" He leered.

"Do you know how old she is?"

"No—but old enough. They grow up at eleven nowadays."

Vernon Grove sat up, slowly. "Did she ask to sit with me?"

"Hell, you conceited bastard, hell no, she didn't." But Doyle's face had turned beet-red and his voice rang out too loud.

"Did any of the other people ask you?"

"No! What *is* all this with you, Grove?" Sputtering and expostulating now, Doyle was grabbing his black trousers from the closet, hauling them on. "They seemed like a decent bunch to me. I figured I was giving you variety. You got the military, the clergy, a very nice guy from Arabia. All high-class people."

"Let me see your lists, Phil." Dr. Grove was leaning forward on the bed. "Gimme." He rubbed his thumb and forefinger together.

"You never bitched about this sort of thing before . . ."

Dr. Grove stood up, again wearing his glassy smile. "Let's have them, Phil . . . the lists."

"What lists? This is nuts, Vernon."

"I want to see exactly what's so great about them. Your *chart* lists." Vernon Grove was breathing heavily. "Why you shoved those morons down my throat . . ."

Doyle looked at him very sharply for a second or two. "Okay," he said. "Okay," he repeated softly.

He jerked open a drawer and produced a sheaf of onion-skin papers, mimeographed seating charts. "Here's your section—Table 3. Here they are," he said.

Vernon Grove leaned against a wall of the vibrating, rattling cabin and read them.

Ellen Stewart and Victoria Graham were from Marshall, Virginia, and Edinburgh, Scotland, respectively. Aunt and niece. In all details their descriptions matched the cards he had been given by Jenkins.

Thomas O'Connor's address was the Holy Name Seminary, Astoria, Queens, Long Island, New York. He was fifty years of age. His occupation was clergyman, R.C.

Omar Aziz hailed from Basra, Iraq.

Robert Ewing and his wife resided at 2 Hibiscus Lane, Fort Lauderdale, Florida. He was described as a retired major in the U.S. Army, and Judy as a housewife.

"Okay?" Doyle asked him, taking back the lists. "They're not bank presidents exactly. But I thought you'd like a change of pace." He gave his quick, sharp smile. "And that kid is crazy about you, so I hear . . . Hell, you don't even eat with 'em most of the time."

"Thanks, Phil." Vernon Grove moved out the door.

"Take a rest, for God's sake. See you at *lunch*," Doyle said.

Bouillon was being served, morning inspection was proceeding as usual, and on this fifth day out, this warm and sunny day, everything looked normal, peaceful, even somnolent. Amy was stretched out at her old post near the flag. Aziz reclined in a deck chair, with his nose in a travel guide. The major was lunging and darting around the ping-pong table. Mrs. Ewing was playing bridge in the lounge. O'Connor was on the sports deck watching shuffleboard.

Only Ellen and her aunt were missing from the scene. Where *did* they spend their days? In that stuffy cabin? He realized that he had not seen Mrs. Graham anywhere since that night at the movies.

Dismissed from inspection, he took a look at the ship's photographs, made of the passengers at their various activities and posted for sale in the main-deck lobby. Neither Ellen nor her aunt was in any of them, but there were several of his other tablemates: of the major and his wife, wearing life-jackets and looking grim at boat drill; of Aziz five mornings ago at embarkation time, walking up the gangplank, grinning; of O'Connor on a sofa in the lounge, with a conglomerate group of old women beaming over bingo: the Ewings at the cocktail-mixer, dancing together; himself and Amy at the cocktail-mixer, dancing: Aziz at bouillon time, craning his neck and smirking in the background with the twin blondes posing in the foreground . . . The pictures taken at the Talent Show the previous night had not yet been developed. But these on display looked very typical run-of-the-mill, as though at least four of his tablemates had been enjoying themselves mightily aboard the *Columbia* and had not given him a second thought.

There was an hour yet to spare till lunchtime. He spent it high on the top deck, standing at the stern and watching the ship's wake, watching the long curling shadow of smoke drift out over the ocean. The supernatural did not exist. Evidence and knowledge had to spring from human beings. And yet five days had passed, and they hadn't laid a finger on him.

Why? Simply because they *knew* he couldn't go anywhere? They could take their time? But it seemed unrealistic. It also seemed totally fantastic that *six* people would spend the money for First Class passages, bribe stewards, use false passports simply to brainwash one wretched suspect—when one simple confrontation would have done the job.

It might even be illegal. Criminals had certain rights these days.

He stared at the horizon and then down at the blue beauty of the water, and wished suddenly that he were fishing in a quiet stream, in a small boat with his son. He had promised the boy so often. He had never taken a vacation in eight years.

At one thirty, when he knew they would be gathered and halfway through the meal, and he would only have half an hour until office hours, he went below, combed his hair, brushed his jacket, and walked briskly toward the elevator.

Stepping from it came Amy. She was bare-legged, wrapped in a robe, and was carrying a towel. Around her head, swathed becomingly, was another towel. "Good *morn*ing, I mean, good after*noon*," she greeted him radiantly.

"You've been swimming, I see," he said.

"Yes. It's such good exercise. Before luncheon," she said. "You're on your way to lunch, Doctor?"

"Yes," he said, stepping into the elevator, pressing the Hold button impatiently.

"Do you ever go swimming, Doctor?"

"Occasionally." He smiled. And then the door slid shut upon her rosy, wistful face.

Doyle was loitering outside the Wedgwood Room. "Congratulations." He grinned. "Have fun. Look gay. After all, it's only two more days, isn't it?"

Vernon Grove grunted, shoved open the leather doors.

Cool, deliciously air-conditioned, the huge bright room, crowded with people, struck him poignantly with its beauty and its elegance. The silver gleamed, the tablecloths were so white, there were flowers in fresh bouquets, and at the portholes the sea was turquoise.

And there at Table 3 was his little family, his happy little family—short of two. Ellen and her aunt were absent.

As he strode forward, looking neither left nor right but only at them, he saw that they had not as yet noticed his entrance. They were all four engaged in earnest conversation, leaning on their elbows, huddled close, but now, as he drew near, the major spotted him, and the other three looked up quickly, looked up as one, breaking off their conversation as if on signal. There seemed no doubt whatever that he had been the subject of their conversation. He could tell, if only by their looks of innocence.

"Well!" the major boomed. "To what do we owe this honor —stranger?" He chuckled.

Dr. Grove smiled. "Sorry," he said, slipping into his chair. "I've never seen it busier."

"We've missed you," O'Connor said.

"Well, so have I, Father," he said. "Ellen's not here?" he asked casually, although it was, of course, perfectly obvious that she was not.

He thought he detected suppressed grins, and it was as though each had the urge to poke his neighbor in the ribs with an insinuating elbow or step on someone's foot under the table. But not Judy Ewing. She was, he now noticed, regarding him with considerably less enthusiasm than were the others, sniffing, as a matter of fact. "No—no," Father O'Connor was saying blandly. "Haven't seen Ellen today." He gazed at the chandelier.

Aziz leaned forward, wriggling with self-importance. "She —sleep," he hissed.

"Never saw a girl need so much sleep," Ewing remarked. "Say! How do you *know* she's asleep, Omar?"

Aziz's dark face grew dark red, and then even Ewing, insensitive though he was, seemed to feel that he had made some sort of blunder. The situation was delicate and complex. It was, after all, Dr. Grove they should be kidding about Ellen.

Like the mingled strains of a string quartet, they then began to talk of the Talent Show, a triumphal post-mortem indeed. They rehashed Aziz's magic tricks (". . . iss nawthing. Mideastern peoples, desert peoples ver' good at treeks") and the Ewings' dancing ("Judy and I took this Fred Astaire course") and Ellen's folk singing (". . . but it took all four of us to persuade her," O'Connor said). Father O'Connor was joshed by Ewing for having no displayable talents. The talk then moved on to the masquerade—heady, exciting event, gala thing, only a few hours away by now.

"I have no *idea* how to dress for it," Judy Ewing said. "Does anybody have any suggestions?"

"I have some, but you wouldn't like them," her husband replied and shook with laughter.

Innocent talk? Guileless people? Ordinary bores, thrown together by chance, by the random stab of a dining-room steward's gold-headed pin?

It was five minutes of two.

"Oh, by the way, Doctor." O'Connor fumbled in his pocket, then laid a colored pamphlet before him with an amiable smile. "Mr. Aziz, you know, is taking a tour of the

Shakespeare country. Do you know anything about this place?"

It was an old soiled advertisement for Glyn Tower.

Creased and discolored, lying there on the tablecloth was a gaudy picture of green lawns with sheep, a pond with statuary, and looming stone towers and battlements. "Fifteenth Century. Five Shillings Admittance," said the caption beneath. And Aziz was leaning across the table toward him, grinning, hissing, "Iss open to publics any more? You know anyssing?"

"No . . . I don't, Mr. Aziz." He rose unsteadily.

"Iss not closed—since murder happen . . . ?"

"No . . . I—I've never heard of it."

"What murder was *that*, Mr. Aziz?" he heard Judy Ewing shrill.

"I read in newspapers . . ."

But Vernon Grove had fled the scene. He heard no more.

During his office hours that sweltering day, Miss Simmons asked him if he felt all right, and he said yes, it was just that he was very tired, and it wasn't as easy as he'd thought, being the only doctor on board, and he wished he could get his hands on Gary Brightwood.

"*Wasn't* it strange the way that happened?" Miss Simmons said. "You know, I'm sure it couldn't have been his mother who called. He didn't *have* a mother. I recall his telling me . . . that she had died the year he entered medical school."

16

HE HAD NOT meant to kill Maida—and he could tell them so.

Several times during the course of that nightmarish afternoon, he was tempted to walk down the corridor to O'Connor's cabin, knock on the door, and make a clean breast of it.

He would throw himself on their mercy, and describe in detail exactly what had happened in Glyn Tower that night. He was *not* a murderer. They were accusing him unjustly.

But who would believe him?

The day darkened. The haze grew thicker. The heat gave way to cold, and a gray and clammy fog began to pervade the ocean. Thick fog floated past his porthole as he stood alone in his cabin at dusk, a man sweating with indecision, turned to ice by fear.

Who would believe that he was innocent—after two years of silence, two years of cowardice?

There had been no eyewitnesses. The castle had been empty—dark, shut up, the electricity turned off, a black, hollow, echoing shell. There had not been one single person present who could prove the truth or falsehood of any statement he might choose to make. And he had *acted* like a murderer.

What had seemed like luck two years ago was now incriminating evidence.

He threw himself down on his bunk, at last, and turned his face to the wall.

He had gone almost crazy that night.

It had been an accident.

Screaming out of the past, he could hear his own voice yelling . . . in that dark, musty bedroom, and the echoes reverberating: "You stupid bitch! Why did you have to *die? Die?*"

He had intended only to push her away, fend her off. It was her fingers moving up and down his arm that had driven him insane. It was her threats, the word "possession" that had cracked him up. But the blow had not been really violent. It was the fall that had killed Maida Jennings, not his blow. Staggering back from him in the dark, she fell, and he heard the crack, the scream, and the sound of sharp wood finding bone.

She stopped screaming, suddenly.

"Maida . . ."

In his hat and raincoat he knelt beside her, and she wasn't breathing. Groping blindly in the clammy dark, he gathered her limp body in his arms and placed her on the bed. He blundered about the room for a light, found a book of matches in her pocketbook, struck one match, then two.

Half naked in the golden dress, she lay across the dark red coverlet, her eyes wide open, staring glassily up at him, and a trickle of blood was oozing from her mouth. Blood was staining the blond hair.

"My God!"

The match burned down to his fingers and went out.

He found the candelabrum and lit three candles. By their flickering light he examined the wound, tried to stanch the blood. It was on the back of her head, near the base of her brain. Obviously, in falling she had struck some sharp projecting corner of one of the huge wardrobes. Even mouth-to-mouth resuscitation didn't help. Nothing helped. She must have died almost instantly.

He straightened up at last, a man of stone, and it was then that he screamed at her, reviled her, and heard the echoes mocking him in that vast, cold, evil house.

His feelings then had been ones of horror and despair—for she had somehow won over him. And now he would never be rid of her. In death she had triumphed.

He would never make his ship in time.

He might never, ever return to the *Columbia.*

He, who had never wanted to come here in the first place, was now trapped with a dead woman. And the police would come and ask him questions. His relationship to her would be exposed. His reputation, his entire way of life would be examined and destroyed. They might even put him in prison, for he had no way of proving that he hadn't killed her deliberately. In cold blood or in a fit of rage. They might charge him with murder in the first degree.

"Damn you! Damn you!"

Holding the candelabrum aloft, he looked at her, and the longer he looked, the more frightful became the impact of those eyes. They seemed to mock him. In the flickering light her lips seemed set in a faint smile.

He bolted out into the hall, kicking the bedroom door shut behind him.

Panting, he stood there, shaking in the deep oppressive silence, the dancing shadows. And the house regarded him, the ancient house with its heritage of cruelty and greed and lust. It was an evil place, and Maida Jennings had been evil.

But what did he owe her now? She was dead—so let her lie here with her evil ancestors. He must get away. He must escape from her. He must get back on board the *Columbia*—in time to sail.

Tiptoeing along, like a shadow, over soft thick carpets, past rooms that were as black and cold as caverns, he reached the wide staircase and inched down it. The golden Buddhas in the hall smiled serenely, unperturbed, as they had smiled for centuries. The suits of armor stood at stiff attention. No one had seen him enter this place, and no one in the world knew where he was. So ran his thoughts as he moved toward the great front door.

"I had a telephone call from someone today that lights had been seen in it," Maida had said, and for a few more minutes he listened, waved the candelabrum to and fro. He heard nothing but the squeak of a mouse scuttling off in the darkness, the sound of the rain outside. He was sure she had made up that excuse on the spot . . . but if she hadn't, then they could blame some local prowler for her death, the footprints, and whatever fingerprints he had left behind. *He'd* be on the high seas by then, out of reach. They'd never suspect him, anyway. They *couldn't* know.

Setting the candelabrum back on the oak table, he wiped it off, however, with his handkerchief, then blew the candles out.

He put his gloves on and opened the front door.

Her little car was still standing where she had left it—on the graveled driveway, with the keys still there. But he merely inspected the bucket seats and floor, to make sure nothing had fallen from his pockets. There was no trace of his presence. Then he rolled the windows down, so that the rain could blow in and wash the interior clean. The rain, falling now in a downpour, would wash his footprints from the gravel, from the lane.

Turning his coat collar up, and giving one last glance at the grim, lightless façade, Maida's mausoleum, he pulled his hat brim low and started running.

He had behaved exactly like a murderer.

Once past the high iron gates, he had struck off blindly through the woods and over fields, and found a faded signpost at last on a lonely country road: "Southampton, 8 Mi." The rain continued and the wind was harsh. The road led him past dripping hedges, in and out of small sleeping settlements, but as he sloshed along through mud or stumbled over wet cobblestones, he encountered no one except a stray dog or two, and they ignored him.

The glow of Southampton, now visible in the sky to the southwest, was still very faint, and his clothes were drenched and clinging to him, when he heard a car approaching. He stepped to one side, but the headlights picked him out, and a truck slowed down, jolted to a standstill. "Like a lift, guv'-nor?" It was a shabby, rattletrap, pickup lorry, and a pasty face was peering out.

"Thank you."

With an explanation all ready on his lips, he climbed into the truck. But the driver had asked him no questions, except for the inevitable "Where you bound for, guv?"

"Southampton," he mumbled, slouching down into the lumpy seat. And beyond this, there had been no further conversation except for "Thank you," and "Good night" at the end of the ride. The man had kept his radio on and seemed completely uninterested. He was transporting lettuces. He was young and stupid-looking. He had a cowlick, and his skin had the consistency of a grated raw potato, but though Dr. Grove studied him, he did not study Dr. Grove at all. They had parted at a dark corner near a market, not far from the docks.

The streets at that hour of a rainy autumn morning were still dark and deserted, the pubs shuttered, silent. From a distance, at the foot of a long slope, he could see the *Columbia* lying at her hawsers, dim-lit, familiar, beautiful. And he had never loved her more. He raced down to her side.

Only an old nightwatchman was on duty at the gangplank. He hadn't seemed surprised to see him. "Had a good night of it, sir?" That was what the old fellow at the gangplank had said, and chuckled after him indulgently, a rasping, tubercular sound. That old man was dead now, dead these many months.

The corridors of the ship had been deserted, silent as the grave, except for distant sounds of hammering, and he fled into his cabin like a harried fox to its hole, locked the door, tore off his wet clothes, rolled them into a ball, and hid them until they were once more out at sea. He had tossed them overboard, at night.

Then he had held his breath, and sweated.

Just as though he were guilty . . . guilty of the crime of murder.

The fog continued to drift past his porthole in ever-thickening gray swirls—this evening in mid-July. It blanketed the ocean and enshrouded the ship with an eerie white stillness, deadening the sounds of the sea, the sense of forward motion. The *Columbia* seemed to hang in limbo. Soon the foghorn began to blast at two-minute intervals, a sound that he had loved since boyhood. And once he had loved fog, he had found it beautiful. But now the horn had a shattering effect. The blind white light unnerved him . . . and the creeping pace of the ship. Even the weather seemed deliberately cruel, evoked especially to remind him of another foggy night.

Maida swung her golden slipper at the bar, and smiled at him. She drew the white glove on, over the big green emerald. She lay staring up at him, with a glassy smile, on a dark red coverlet.

He must sleep. He had to have some rest. He swallowed two tranquilizers.

He closed his eyes and drew the covers up over his head. *Nobody* could possibly blame him, and *nobody* had been there. The case had been officially closed. He had read everything there was to know about it.

Maida's body hadn't even been discovered for three or four days, which proved that no one could have witnessed her death. Not until a maid came in to air the rooms had anybody missed her from her flat, or even known that she had gone to Glyn Tower.

They had suspected the gardener—whose salary was long overdue.

They had picked up a tramp in nearby Salisbury, and questioned him.

They had interviewed her friend, Miss Josephine Ludlow, who was "prostrate with grief, under heavy sedation," but the distracted Miss Ludlow couldn't offer them any clues. "Everybody liked her," she was quoted in the British tabloids (which Vernon Grove purchased surreptitiously in Southampton or on 42nd Street). "She was talented and generous." Miss Ludlow did not mention any shipboard romance. She seemed to have ignored it—and have done so, bless her, ever since.

Maida's telephone book in Chelsea was examined.

His name was obviously not in it. He *had* no phone number except the *Columbia,* and she had just arrived in London the night before.

Foreign movie stars and beatniks, beach boys from Majorca, sheepherders and pimps, even her Indian connections had popped in and out of the newspapers as the weeks crawled by. But from voyage to voyage the items had shrunk, and gradually a curious picture of Maida had emerged. She had lived a brilliant, spendthrift life, traveled incessantly, dabbled in everything, but there had never been a single serious love affair, no man who had ever had much to do with her. *He* had been the only one, perhaps, the only one who had encouraged her, the match that set the tinder aflame.

By the Christmas season of 1964, however, when the *Columbia* made her annual holiday cruise to the Caribbean, the police seemed to have given up on her, and there were no more items—in Kingston, St. Thomas, or Trinidad. He found nothing in New York in January, 1965, nothing in England in February and March. She had vanished from the public mind. She was ancient history. She was just another unsolved crime—or accident—among thousands. He had seen no reference to the case for a year and a half.

The engines pulsed, the foghorn boomed. He hadn't meant to kill her—and any sensible jury, any clear-thinking judge would realize that. A good lawyer would get him off. British justice was very fair. In English courts the judges and the lawyers wore wigs, old eighteenth-century wigs, that made them look ridiculous . . .

From the depths of sleep he heard a phone ringing. It sounded far off, remote, at first, as if it were ringing in some distant room, in some other time . . . in his childhood flat, his mother's flat in Brooklyn, and out in the Narrows a passing ship was blasting its foghorn. Then he knew that it was ringing right next to his ear.

"Yes?" he answered thickly.

"Vern? Is that you, Vern? What's wrong with your voice?" It was Jenkins. "What the hell are you doing? It's ten o'clock."

"Ten o'clock . . ." he repeated dazedly.

"The masquerade, for God's sake. Get up here. I can't handle all this alone. Kick that woman out of your bed and get your costume on."

Vernon Grove let his head fall back on the pillow. "Listen, Bob," he said, "I don't think I can make it. I'm whipped. I feel lousy. It's unjust . . ."

"Okay, so we're all whipped. We *all* feel lousy. There are a thousand people up here, and it's a *great* night at sea," Jenkins croaked. "Listen." His tone became ominous. "Anderson was asking where you were. He came through here ten minutes ago."

"Anderson? I don't believe it." But Vernon Grove stiffened.

"I swear to God. He was right here, asking who the judges were, and I told him, and he said where the hell were you, why hadn't you reported, and to get this clambake on the *road*, for God's sake. So, come on, Vern, or he'll be calling you."

Jenkins slammed down the phone.
The foghorn blasted.

Vernon Grove reached for his bedside lamp and switched it
on. He sat on the edge of the bed, looking at the floor. The
sleep had done him no good. It had made him feel worse—a
strange, troubled sleep that had left him with a throbbing
headache, a deeper sense of doom and misery.

Shaking his head, he got to his feet, surveyed his supply of
drugs, swallowed two headache tablets, and then, two Dexedrines.

Then he hauled his costume from the closet, the same costume he had worn at every masquerade for the past six years.
It was the authentic dress of a male Spanish dancer. He had
bought it from an Andalusian waiter years ago, and it had
once been dashing: tight pants, high-heeled leather boots, and
a stiff-brimmed black hat. The women had often told him it
set off his blue eyes and blond hair. They had gone wild over
the combination.

Now it was a trifle worn, a little too tight, and the shirt had
not been laundered this week. He had forgotten to give it to
his room steward.

His eyes were bloodshot and his face was the texture of
chalk. He had never looked worse. Standing before the mirror, though, he tilted the sombrero at the proper slant and
drew the chin cord tight. Then, squaring his shoulders, he
swung open the door. The tight pointed boots went clicking
through the empty corridors.

17

BLARING MUSIC vied with the steady booming of the foghorn.

As he approached the lounge he could hear the rhythmic shuffle of many feet. Standing at the doorway unsteadily, peering in, he could see only fantastic headgear and painted faces bobbing by under balloons and streamers in the dim blue light. The air was thick with smoke and reeked with the odor of many bodies. Past the distant windows floated gray dense fog. It was like looking into hell, witnessing a dance of demons.

"Thank God, Vern. Congratulations." The purser hauled him inside. "Start mingling. Look 'em over. I've still gotta get the damned prizes wrapped." He dived away.

Everybody on board seemed to be in the salon, dancing, milling aimlessly, or seated at the tables that were ranged around the sides of the dance floor. The fog had driven them up from their staterooms to noise and gaiety, the foghorn had frightened them with its overtones, reminiscent of the *Titanic* and the *Andrea Doria*. At the last minute they had gone burrowing about in their suitcases, or driven the stewards crazy for some makeshift prop. He saw the blondes dance by dressed as Playboy bunnies, Indians in ship's blankets, angels in sheets, mummies swathed in toilet paper.

But Ellen was wearing a real costume.

She was in a distant corner, seated at a table near a window—with Aziz, in his turban and magician's robe, and the Ewings, who were wearing their Charleston costumes. Her back was toward him. She was dressed as a witch, the long red hair flowing from a black high-peaked hat and over a black flowing robe, a very grotesque outfit, certainly out of character. He could not see her face, but she seemed to be wearing a mask, something white, with a hooked nose no doubt. She disgusted him. He turned his back and made his way to the opposite corner. He stepped behind a pillar and looked again.

They were all talking very animatedly. Aziz was whispering in Ellen's ear. The peaked hat was nodding and nodding.

"Hi there! Is it authentic?" A bright gay voice addressed him and a light hand touched his bolero. "I've been *wondering* if that was you. What a *delightful* combination. It's just fascinating . . . with your blue eyes."

Amy Harrison was standing at his side, dressed as Cleopatra, svelte as a reed—and drunk. She giggled. "I have a thing about flamenco. Are those *real* flamenco boots?" She was wearing a black chiffon nightgown, heavy eye make-up, and a brilliant smile.

"Yes," he said.

In her hair were golden asps, made of cardboard, which quivered as she swayed before him. "Can you dance the way Antonio does? All that stamping, and the *beautiful* posture?" She threw her head back, thrust her bosom out, and stamped her feet. She clicked her fingers. "Oh, I've never gotten over Spain." She laughed, then put her hands on his shoulders. "*Dance* with me, please. It's a samba. Please?"

He took her in his arms and danced close to the pillar. The castanets, the maracas were barely audible above the noise.

"Are you cross with me about something, Doctor? Hm?" She cuddled closer, raised the big brown painted eyes.

"No. Of course not."

He kept watching Ellen, over Amy's head, but she had not yet turned. She was still whispering to Aziz.

"Really? You seem awfully aloof. I haven't seen you to talk to . . . since that evening at the movies. I keep feeling that *I* must have done something."

"Not at all, Amy. I've been busy, that's all. Up to my neck."

"*Have* you?" she said. And her eyes were following him, following his gaze. "I saw the way that beautiful little girl was looking at you last night at the Talent Show. And you were whispering together. Are you very fond of her?"

"No! For—for Pete's sake, Mrs. Harrison!"

"It's Amy," she said, smiling. She pressed her head against his chest again. "Well, the cruise is almost over, isn't it," she murmured dreamily. "I'll always remember how nice you were to me. You were really sweet."

She lay in his arms heavily. Her legs brushed his. And her body was so soft and warm. She had practically nothing on underneath that nightgown. The first woman's body he had held in a week.

"It was a pleasure," he mumbled. "I'm sorry it's over. Maybe we could get together sometime . . . somewhere . . . in my quarters."

"Really?" She lifted glazed bright eyes. "When?"

"Oh—maybe tomorrow sometime." He ducked his head in the black hat. "Where are you getting off, Le Havre or Southampton?"

"Southampton," she said. "Tomorrow will be my final evening . . ."

"Well, fine. Tomorrow . . ." His voice trailed off vacantly. His attention had just been caught by something just beyond Ellen's tall peaked hat, outside the window, out on deck.

Amy was asking him some question, but he could not cope with it. His mind was groping with a curious vision which had just flickered past that window, and now was gone.

Something shimmering. Something gold.

"Is that all right, Doctor?"

"Yes," he said.

The light turned yellow. The music ended. And it was back. It was standing right there, for an instant, at that window again, and in the brighter light pouring from the pane he could see its outline—the outline of a woman in a golden dress, with golden hair.

It vanished. The fog rolled over it.

"What's the matter?" said Amy. "Does the prospect frighten you?" She laughed up into his face, then stared. "You look so pale, Doctor."

"It's okay, okay," he muttered hoarsely.

Two Dexedrines, two tranquilizers, and no sleep were responsible for that thing outside.

"Let me buy you a drink. Let *me* treat *you* . . ." She took his hand. She tried to drag him to the bar—toward Harry the crocodile, toward the place where Ellen and the others were still sitting. But he stood his ground and shook his head, his eyes fixed only on the windows now. If he saw it again, he would know that it was not an illusion. He would know exactly what it was.

"You *need* a drink . . ."

She could not be Ellen Stewart. She did not resemble any woman he had ever known, save one. Her hair was shoulder-length, loose and swinging. Her dress was metallic. Standing out there in the fog, at a portside window now, her back turned to him, she was brandishing a long cigarette holder.

"Excuse me . . ."

He did not stop to think. He left Amy standing there and fought his way through the crowd.

He was greeted by the foghorn. Hoarse and harsh, deep-toned and prolonged, it was deafening in the cold dank mist. The *Columbia* was bellowing like an angry bull to the shroud of fog, the invisible ocean: bellowing a warning. Puffs of fog flew past his eyes. The damp wind pierced his flimsy shirt.

He stood for a second, looking for a shimmer of gold, listening for the tap of heels. In the thick mist he could see nothing but the faint outline of the rail, the fuzzy blur of the ship's lights, hear nothing but the sound of the engines and the rush of the sea.

Still dazed by all the drugs he had consumed, he began to tiptoe cautiously, keeping in close against the walls of the lounge, edging past the windows. Inside, bathed in the blue light, the dancers glided past the panes like fish in an aquarium. But peering in, he managed to spot Ellen's table, Ellen's tall peaked hat and Aziz's turban. They had not moved. They were not following him.

Moving out close to the rail, he began to follow it toward the forward end of the ship. The fog was blinding. Distances were deceiving, perspective gone, but then, ahead, he thought he saw her, a golden blur, standing near a window, and now, at the sound of his footsteps, turning and moving off.

"Hey!"

She had disappeared . . . but he had heard the light tap of high heels scuttling off into the fog.

Real footsteps.

He stood, hesitating a moment, and then, in the tight leather boots, he began to jog along the slippery deck, the leather heels beating a loud tattoo, but when he reached the stern, there was no sign of her, no sound.

The foghorn jeered.

He stood there, listening to his heartbeat and the dying echoes of the foghorn, and when the echoes stopped, he was sure he heard the faint tap-tap of footsteps above his head. Nearby was an iron-runged companionway. Grasping it, and straining his eyes, he thought that he could faintly discern a dark blur up there on the sports deck, standing by the rail, then vanishing. The foghorn hooted again as he climbed the slippery rungs in pursuit.

At the top, he paused to listen again, and hearing nothing, he moved warily into the dense fog, thicker up here than it had been below. Something fell with an enormous clatter. He had knocked over a shuffleboard pole that was leaning against a ventilator. Cursing, he moved on, until he felt cold wet mesh pressed against his face. Recoiling, he reached out and touched the volley-ball net that somebody had forgotten to take down. He grabbed it, tore at it in fury, and the poles supporting it fell to the deck.

Again he paused to listen, and now, high above, up in the kennel area on the top deck, he heard the sudden uproar of dogs barking, dogs aroused by the clatter of the falling poles— or by someone up there, passing their cages.

The barking subsided, and then rose again, floating in an eerie chorus out over the sea. He plodded up the last companionway then. His sombrero had been knocked from his head when he ran into the volley-ball net and now lay back over his shoulders, held by the chin cord. His shirt, the short bolero jacket were sopping.

Reaching the top deck, he began groping blindly along, past the kennels and the whining dogs, past the lifeboats swinging from their davits, past the misty lights, feeling, groping, breathing heavily.

He touched something. It was soft . . . a woman's body.

The dress was not metallic. It was white—and sodden.

The hair was long, waist-length.

She was standing pressed against one of the giant funnels, perfectly still, scarcely breathing, and her face was deathly pale, her eyes were fixed, wide open, staring past him.

"Ellen!"

She did not stir. She made no sound.

"Ellen, what the hell is this?"

She stood as still as stone.

"Hey! Wake up! Snap out of it. It's me." He snapped his fingers before her eyes. "What's wrong with you?"

He shook her arm.

She stared into space, ignoring him.

"I didn't realize it was you I was chasing," he said in a jocular tone. "I thought you were wearing a witch's costume. I was wrong."

No reaction. Her expression remained a perfect blank.

"Come *on.* What's this act? Lay off it, Ellen. I'm not dumb."

She stared vaguely down at the arm he was squeezing, as though it were a separate thing, and then turned her gaze back to the fog.

There was a total absence of fear about her, only a strange vacant calm, like a sleepwalker or a catatonic, and he stepped back now and surveyed her up and down intently. Then he said bitterly, "What did you do down there? Throw the other dress overboard? And the wig? I *knew* that it was you."

No answer. No alarm.

"What are you trying to prove?" he shouted.

The foghorn bellowed in reply. It hooted at him—and his nerves, he knew, were beginning to snap. But then he had a sudden inspiration.

"Come on, baby . . ." He took her by her slender shoulders. "Stop this childish bit. I know all about it—so—let's call it quits." He wrenched her close and kissed her full on the mouth.

His hands were moving over a limp rag doll. Her lips were warm and lifeless.

"God! You *bitch!*" He released her furiously, and she staggered back against the funnel. He could hear the sound of her head striking metal.

"Damn you!"

She was righting herself, beginning to drift away.

"No! You aren't going anywhere!" Seizing the limp hand, he spun her around to him. *"Talk!* Damn it. *Answer* me! Do you hear me? *Say* something!"

She stared at him, wide-eyed and mute.

"I'll make you talk!"

And now, feeling only the blood boiling in his head, all the pent-up fury and madness of the past insane days, he shook her, then his fingers moved to her throat. He could feel its softness. He could feel the throbbing and the fluttering of the veins. He pressed.

"Do you want to die? Do you? Do you?" he panted hoarsely.

"Dr. Grove?" said a low, quiet voice from the shadows. "Dr. Grove, is that you, Doctor?" It was right behind him. With a yell he turned around, and there, creeping up behind him, was the tall gaunt figure of the witch, the tall peaked hat, the long black robe. "To whom are you speaking?" she asked. "Who's there?"

"Your niece . . ."

"My niece?" She was without her mask, without her spectacles. Her dark eyes darted through the fog at him, her smile was malicious. "My niece Ellen is in her cabin *sleeping*," she said in the modulated, precise tones. "She is not well. She *sees* things." She raised one skinny arm. "Evil spirits that walk the night. And hellfire." The dark eyes blazed.

He stood there, staring at her. Ellen had slipped away.

"Do you see things, too, Dr. Grove?" She peered into his face, and her breath was foul. "You commune with spirits?" Hollowly she smiled and touched his wrist with chilly fingers. "Then I pity you, I pity you . . ." She stalked away, theatrically, into the mist.

And then he knew, at least, who *she* was.

He knew the full power of his enemies.

It had only been a fleeting resemblance and he had never really looked at the woman, but standing there in the fog, shaking and sodden, and sickened to the core, he had no doubt that Mrs. Graham was Miss Josephine Ludlow. Once again Maida's actress friend had stepped aboard the S.S. *Columbia*, and was occupying Cabin B54.

18

SOMETIME in the very early morning, before it was light, he had a phone call. "Yes?" He assumed it was Miss Murphy, who was covering that night. He had told her to screen every call, to check with him before putting it through.

The voice was a woman's, unfamiliar, high-pitched, faint. The only words he could make out were "Doctor, Doctor." The rest was gibberish.

He replaced the receiver. Almost instantly the phone rang again. It was the same shrill, distant voice. "Doctor, Doctor!" she cried, and the sound was as remote, as unintelligible as the squealing of a seagull. It kept fading, dying, shrieking with sudden volume again, a jabber rising and falling. "To hell with you," he muttered, and slammed the receiver down.

He lay there, sweating on the bed, with muscles taut. The phone rang at least three times more, but he did not answer it. He lay there, watching the dawn of this next to last day now, thinking as he'd thought for hours about Josephine Ludlow. Thinking what a fool he'd been ever to trust her, not even to recognize her six days ago, not to realize that only a woman could have devised this hellish frame-up job, masterminded this torture.

That O'Connor and Aziz and the Ewings were in it as well,

he was still perfectly sure, but Miss Ludlow had to be the leading spirit. *She* had known about his relationship with Maida, and had gone about quietly collecting facts (from the truck driver? the garage attendant? Maida's Chelsea neighbors?), putting two and two together, needling the police—and coaching Ellen. This entire hoax smacked of a jealous, bitter, ruthless woman—and a theatrical one. He had it all down pat—at last. It explained the pettiness, the nerve-racking quality of this maniacal campaign. And as for not recognizing her, it was the easiest thing in the world for a middle-aged actress to make up as an old woman. Time and grief had also aged her, perhaps. Vengeance and purpose had burned the flesh off her portly frame and possibly turned the dark hair gray. She had taken a chance, coming back to her old cabin, but he had been deceived, simply because she had stayed out of his sight so long.

The phone rang again, and at six o'clock he heard a rapping on his waiting-room door and Miss Murphy's voice outside. "Doctor, doctor, are you in there? *Please* open up."

When he unlocked the door, she asked, "Isn't your phone connected?"

"What about *your* phone?" he asked. He was sure that she had been with Doyle.

She reddened. "I've been trying to reach you for the past hour, Doctor, and you didn't answer. Some woman in Tourist says her child is sick. She can't speak any English. Doctor, are you ill? You look just awful. And you're still in your costume . . ."

Armed with stethoscope and lollipops, he went below—to the depths of the *Columbia*, following dark, narrow, stuffy corridors to the small cheap accommodations of Tourist Class. The ship still slept. As he descended, the engine noises grew louder and the air more close. He knocked on the door of a tiny cubicle, one about the size of a First Class bathroom.

"Mrs. Organy? I'm the ship's doctor."

Mrs. Organy was very young, very pregnant, and she spoke no English. Her voice was high-pitched, unintelligible. The sick child was a little boy, with flaming cheeks and feverish eyes, lying in a lower bunk. On the upper bunk perched a still younger boy, probably four years old, who was sucking his thumb. The cabin was draped with laundry, crowded with suitcases.

Vernon Grove examined the sick child. He had swollen tonsils.

"He's all right." Grimacing, nodding, pointing to his throat, he tried to make her understand. He produced some pills, pointed to the directions. *"Parlez-vous français? Deutsch? Espagnol?"* She had brown hair, nervous blue eyes, and he couldn't figure out her nationality. She kept shaking her head, standing there with her bulging belly in the flowered housecoat, and he wondered how she had managed to get this far alone, or even had the nerve to try.

"Hungarian," piped a little voice from aloft. And the boy had removed his thumb from his mouth. "I tell the Momma." And he scrambled down from the bunk, a merry, agile little fellow with a round tow head. "Missus help us."

"Who's Missus?" He laughed, and was startled by the sound. It was the first time he had laughed in days.

"Next-door lady." The child took the pills from his hands, grinned and nodded.

"What's your name, buddy?" He rumpled the blond hair.

"Anton—Or-*gany.*"

"Well, you're a *good* boy, Anton," Vernon Grove said. The child's hair felt very soft and very, very clean. "Like a lollipop?" He pulled one from his bag. "One for your brother too, when he gets better?"

"Thank you, mister."

"Goodbye, Anton." He eyed the woman's swollen belly again, and smiled. "Goodbye, good luck, ma'am."

She murmured something that sounded like "Drschk," and closed the door behind him.

Thus began the longest, most unreal of all the days that had passed, a day whose unreality was emphasized by the miraculous beauty of the weather: a day so bright, so clear and so translucent it was as though the *Columbia* had sailed overnight from hell into paradise. Every trace of fog had vanished. The air was so transparent and pure one could taste it on the tongue. One could see across the ocean for miles, and even imagine the green coast of France on the blue horizon, though Le Havre was still a day's journey away.

The ship moved like a huge white castle in the morning light. She cast a great gliding shadow on the sea. Marching on stiff legs with the morning-inspection group, Vernon Grove saw nothing of his tablemates.

He saw only the signs of departure, preparation—and farewell that morning. Though the ship would not arrive in Le Havre till after midnight, and not reach Southampton until three of the following day, change was in the air. Steamer trunks were standing outside cabin doors, waiting to be tagged. Suitcases were being packed, hangers were clattering. Stewards and stewardesses were being extra attentive. In the lounges there was feverish camaraderie. Queues were being formed in front of the purser's cubicle for boat-train tickets to Paris, to London, and the exchange of dollars for francs and pounds and shillings.

He marched along, making his own farewells to the *Columbia*.

Farewell the flag that had fluttered and flapped its way across the ocean for eight years—and to the pretty faces that had bobbed up invariably, like keys on a piano. Farewell the bouillon, his old, trusty conversation piece—and farewell the Game. Farewell to ease and status, gleaming uniforms and elegant living. At any moment these would be no more, and he would never walk these decks again.

A lump rose in his throat and a sob welled in his chest. It was abominable. His fingers clenched and unclenched at his side.

The bright wind blew. The white ship sparkled. At the end of inspection, Mr. Anderson turned around, paused and seemed to study him with a sorrowful eye. The chief exec, in fact, seemed on the point of speaking, but then he turned his broad back brusquely, marched away with heavy tread.

Vernon Grove ate lunch that day with the kitchen help.

After he had inspected the kitchens, he perched on a stool and asked one of the chefs to make him a sandwich and some iced coffee.

"You not feeling so good today, Doc?" the chef asked.

"Sure, but I'm getting fat," he said. "Going on a diet."

"I hear you've missed a lot of meals already this trip," said the chef. "Not like you, Doc." He chuckled.

Vernon Grove sat there amidst the clatter of pots and pans,

the clouds of rising steam, watching dishes being washed and waiters hurrying in and out with silver trays. He watched the preparations already being made for tonight's captain's dinner, the trip's last gala meal, a Lucullan banquet. Dough was being rolled out and fluted, meringues were being twirled into fantastic creations, bloody carcasses were being butchered, and a hundred little naked guinea hens lay stuffed and trussed, all ready for the oven—and for stomachs stretched already to the bursting point.

His table waiter spied him, and approached him. "You not coming in again today, Doctor?" the man asked.

"No. Not today, John."

John shifted his tray. He smiled unpleasantly. "They'll be awfully disappointed, Doctor. Particularly the young lady." He grinned again and scurried off.

Vernon Grove left half his sandwich and returned to his cabin. He threw himself across the bed. It was a quarter of two. When Miss Simmons arrived, he was still there, face down. "Is there anything the matter, Doctor? Are you ill or something?"

"No. Just exhausted," he said. "I've got to get some sleep, Elsie. Do you think you could take over for me just this once—you and Mrs. Levy? For a while, anyway? I've been up since dawn."

"Well, of *course*, Doctor," she said. "You aren't looking well."

"Thanks. And take all messages.'"

"There was one this morning," she said, "while you were out. A Mrs. Harrison. She said it wasn't too important. You could call her back."

"Well, thanks, Elsie."

Sleep came in great gulps, mercifully, like oxygen to an

asphyxiated man. He drank it in, and for two blissful hours Dr. Grove lay sprawled there in the sunlight of his paneled bedroom, deaf to the commotion, the comings and goings in the room beyond. The sun had moved a couple of inches, and the light was cooler, when a timid knock and Miss Simmons' urgent whisper awakened him.

She tiptoed in and stood above him, looking embarrassed and flustered.

"Dr. Grove, I hate to disturb you, but we're absolutely swamped today. *Everybody* is here. As usual. And they all want checkups, or a word with you. They're getting out of hand."

He could hear the hum beyond, from the waiting room— the presence of many people. On the sixth day out one might have known that it would be this way. There was even a certain stridency. Either because they were bent on squeezing the last free item from their tickets, or they were panicky at the thought of Europe and its unknown perils, every last Tom, Dick, and Harry scurried up here to have their hearts checked, their stomachs checked, and to obtain free remedies for diarrhea, constipation, sore feet, insomnia, or free advice on the drinking water and the women of the Continent.

He rose from his bed wearily and donned his white coat.

"Yes, madam. What can I do for you?" It was four thirty. Five. "Next, please?"

This day was passing. He could still not believe it. After last night's encounters he could not understand why he was being left alone.

At twenty minutes to six Amy Harrison telephoned. "How are *you*, Doctor? Busy? You hadn't called me back, so—"

Her voice was tentative, breathless, and he couldn't quite figure out why. "Are you all right? Really? You didn't come back to the masquerade. I didn't see you."

"No. I had a patient." Most of his encounter with her last night was just a blur, part of a horrible dream.

"I want to apologize for my behavior," she said, still breathlessly. "I'm afraid I had just a little bit too much to drink."

"Oh, that's all right. I wasn't even aware of it."

"No?"

"No, Amy."

There were no more people in the waiting room. He could hear the quiet, and Miss Simmons and Mrs. Levy seemed to have stepped out. All he wanted was to hang up on her now, get up and shut that door, lock it tight.

"Then you are still expecting me?" she asked.

"Expecting you?"

There was a silence. Then her voice came on—cool and tremulous. "Maybe I'm mixed up," she said. "Maybe I had too much to drink. But I—I had the *impression*, Doctor, that you had invited me to have a drink with you, in your office this evening."

"Oh," he said. He could remember nothing of their conversation.

"It isn't a bit important . . ."

"Oh no," he said hastily. "It *is* . . ."

"It's simply that some *other* friends had invited me for a little farewell celebration," continued the soft, slightly quavering voice, "and I ought to let them know."

"Yes. Certainly," he said, staring now across the black and white linoleum.

Ellen Stewart was standing in the doorway of his examining room, looking in.

"It's quite all right, Doctor. They are charming people. Well, goodbye, Doctor. *Au revoir* . . ."

Around her throat was a white chiffon scarf. And she was smiling, fingering it.

"Wait a minute, Amy," he said. "Don't go. May I call you back in couple of minutes? Ten minutes? Don't decide . . ."

"Well, certainly."

And the receiver clicked. Ellen walked toward him slowly —her great green eyes on his.

"It *hurts* . . ." That was the first thing she said to him. But her face was still smiling as she undid the scarf, and he saw the black and blue marks, the bruises on her throat. She was dressed in the white shift, now immaculate, and her brilliant hair shimmered in the dying sun. "I don't know how . . . um . . . it happened," she said, the green eyes wide and childlike. "Do you suppose it could have happened in my . . . um . . . *sleep*, Doctor?" She moved tentatively to the examining table.

"I don't know. Let's take a look at it," he managed to say. He gestured her to a stool.

"I . . . um . . . had this terrible dream." She sank before him, smiling timidly. "And it was so very f-frightening. I keep thinking that I . . . um . . . um . . . might have injured myself . . . um . . . during the night, against the . . . um . . . bed, or even tried to . . . um . . . pinch myself, or choke myself awake. Do you think that's . . . um . . . possible, Doctor? I know I didn't leave the cabin all night long . . ."

"Hm. Let's see." He studied the marks of his fingers on her

neck. He looked her in the eye. "You say you didn't leave the cabin all night, Ellen?"

"Yes. I went to sleep around eight o'clock," she answered sweetly. "I was so tired. Aunt Victoria wanted me to go to the masquerade with her, but I didn't feel like it."

God!

Her eyes were gentle, trusting, totally devoid of fear.

"I see. Well—let's put some ointment on it."

"Oh, *thank* you . . . What wonderful hands you have, Doctor. Strong but gentle."

Applying the ointment, his hands trembled, but her eyes kept glowing at him and her body relaxed under his touch.

"That'll do it," he said. "Okay. And I'll give you the jar."

"*Thank* you." She rose gracefully.

He led the way to the door. "Just put it on again, some more tomorrow." There was no one in the waiting room, not a living soul. "Okay, Ellen. Have fun this evening. And you can put some powder or make-up over that stuff, if you like."

"Oh, can I? Is it . . . um . . . safe?" she caroled.

"Perfectly safe if the powder is antiseptic. Well—see you later, Ellen."

But she remained rooted to the linoleum.

"Then you are . . . um . . . coming to the captain's dinner?" she asked softly. "You are joining us?"

"I *hope* so. Sure." He nodded, twitched another smile, and pushed the door leading to the waiting room a little wider.

"I am . . . um . . . wearing a new dress," she breathed. "A cocktail dress. And Major Ewing is treating to champagne. I have never *drunk* champagne." She came forward now, and stood beside him. Every nerve in his body was jumping, crawling. "You *will* come? You . . . um . . . promise?"

"Promise." He moved on.

"*Please* do." She moved with him. "You see—I haven't seen you—for a minute since the Talent Show. And I—I *am* becoming different. Don't you see the difference?" She looked up into his face with open guileless eyes.

"No, not really," he said. "But we'll talk about it later, okay?" He swung the waiting-room door open on the silent corridor. "Miss Simmons?" he called.

"Even the night steward noticed it," she breathed. "Last night, when I woke up from my dream, around one in the morning, I went to the door of the cabin to look for Aunt Victoria, and *he* was there, and he looked *scared*." With the rapid delivery she had used several times, she added shakily, "He said, 'Oh my goodness, miss, I thought you was somebody *else* for a minute.' But he couldn't remember her name, only that he had seen her in that cabin, yes, isn't that . . . um . . . awful?"

"Eddie said that? Eddie? I don't believe it . . ."

But it was hopeless to argue, insane to argue.

"And *I'm* changing. I can . . . um . . . feel it. She is struggling—to *possess* me." Emphasizing the word "possess," she clutched his arm, and gazing one more moment into his eyes with a look of horror, she fled his waiting room.

And two minutes later Miss Simmons came in.

"All finished up, Doctor?" She was briskly rubbing her red raw hands. "That was quick—and thank you. I'd have been here until eight."

"Where were you?" he barked.

"Oh, I just ran out to powder my nose a minute. There was nobody left . . ." She eyed him. "Doctor, you don't look a bit good. You'd better get right back into that bed."

"No." He turned his back on her. "Who's on duty this evening?"

"Mrs. Levy."

"Okay. Will you tell her, please, that I'm not to be disturbed. I'm expecting an important guest."

19

CLAWING desperately for reality, seeking something familiar, Vernon Grove phoned Amy Harrison back, and then rang for his room steward. He swung into action— and action felt good.

His examining table was pushed against the wall, covered with a cloth, and the linoleum was swept and mopped. Chairs, a loveseat and a coffee table, a couple of extra lamps were brought in from the waiting room and arranged in an intimate group on one side of the office. His bed was remade, everything was tidied, and the air was sprayed with a pine-scented bomb.

These preparations, this time-honored ritual were restorative, a stimulus in themselves, a welcome distraction. They were also proof of his coolness, his nonchalance to others— and to himself. Like Beau Brummell, dying alone in poverty in Paris but dressing in court finery every night, he felt that he was behaving with heroic *sang-froid* in the very jaws of adversity. Besides, he had begun to think of Amy almost superstitiously by now: she had been sent to him by Providence. She might prove his good-luck charm.

So, down to the last detail, even to the selection of certain suitable records for his hi-fi set which would provide the proper subliminal musical accompaniment for this tryst, he gave his acute attention, and some zeal. At six forty-five Victor brought the menu up.

The very sight of Victor in this cabin cheered him.

Victor was Vernon Grove's favorite waiter, a Roumanian, with a pin-line mustache and a habitual air of hauteur. For eight years Victor had served him—on these gala evenings—discreetly, devotedly. These charming, intimate dinner parties had given free rein to Victor's artistic tastes in food and his love for all the details of high living.

Maida had said he might have stepped out of Mayerling.

"The usual?" Victor asked tonight, glancing around the rooms with unspoken swift approval.

"The usual. What would you recommend, Victor?"

"I would suggest the chateaubriand. The guinea hen, it is so-so. Petits pois. Endive au roquefort. The zabaglione, if you wish dessert . . ."

"Splendid," Vernon Grove nodded solemnly.

"And the wine, Doctor?"

"Would you select one for me, please, Victor?"

"May I suggest a vintage I myself have imported . . . from a vineyard near Nîmes. It is full-bodied, exquisite."

"Very good," Vernon Grove said. "And a shaker of vodka martinis, please."

Victor stalked out, aquiver with self-importance, clearly delighted to have the doctor back on the job. And not once had the presence of a lady, or indeed the existence of any lady, been mentioned between them—nor had it ever been in the past eight years. But Victor's activities and mission would be known in the kitchens. They would not remain unknown to Doyle—or to the rest of the ship's grapevine. All those sneaks and connivers would know that Vernon Grove was totally indifferent to their treachery, and entertaining regally tonight.

He then anointed himself.

He showered and shaved, and changed to a fresh uniform. Brushing his hair before the mirror, he was struck anew by the haggard face looking back at him. But Amy would restore its glow. Every inch the spruce young officer, the polished host, he was pacing up and down his quarters by seven fifteen, straightening a chair, fingering an ashtray, glancing at his watch.

The sunset that evening was vivid, extraordinarily brilliant. It poured through his porthole, painting walls, linoleum, and ceilings a Pompeiian hue. Gorgeous crimsons, oranges dripped from tinctured clouds, and the colors spread across the entire sky. The sea reflected them. The ocean was stained the color of blood.

At seven thirty precisely, Amy arrived.

She wore a black cocktail frock, very short, low-cut, with the thinnest of shoulder straps. She was painted, perfumed, and lacquered. Petite, exquisite, she was a doll out of tissue paper. Her eyes sparkled brilliantly. She danced into the bright pink dusk.

"How charming. How *attractive*. I had no idea. Vodka martinis! You *remembered!*" She swayed over to the loveseat. She sat perched on it, smiling. She surveyed the room with that intent, feverish smile which he had seen on so many women in his time. She filled the silence with her soft, cultured chatter.

"*La mer?* Oh, I adore it. What a perfectly beautiful sky."

In the fading pink light they sat together before the silver platter of shrimp, and made the usual preliminary small talk. "I must apologize for the way I acted at the masquerade, Doctor. But I have a thing about fog. I simply *loathe* it."

He nodded, listened to her, refilled her glass.

In the gathering dusk her posture became more languorous.

In the deepening shadows she confessed to him that life at
times seemed dull and meaningless to her. These last six days
at sea had brought her strange new perspectives, somehow, on
life and on herself. "I suppose it's been being quite alone," she
said—as they always said. "I found that I was not quite as
stuffy . . . or as smug." She did not mention her husband at
all. They never did at this stage of the Game. After six days of
new perspectives Edward Harrison was blurred, fading into
oblivion. He'd return, in time, but meanwhile she wasn't even
twirling the diamond ring any more, she was twirling her martini glass.

Things were going just as they had always gone.

Not a man ever inclined to propel the moment too precipi-
tately to a climax, a man who had always preferred to savor
rather than to lunge, Vernon Grove stuck to his time
schedule, and continued to sip Scotch.

There was also the consideration that every moment spent
here was one moment more spent away from Table 3. It was
now eight thirty. The captain's dinner would by now be
raucously under way. It gave him bitter pleasure just to think
of them all down there, under the balloons and streamers, in
funny paper hats, with champagne corks popping and metal
horns honking, glowering at his empty chair.

"Freshen it up?" he asked.

"Oh, *thank* you, though I shouldn't." She giggled. "But *do*
tell me something about yourself, Doctor. I seem to be doing
all the talking . . ."

"There's nothing very much to tell." He launched into the
familiar lines. "I've lived a pretty dull life, a lonely life. Lots

of hard work, very little relaxation."

"Oh, I can't believe it. You're so young—and so attractive." The martinis were beginning to show. "Have you *never* married?"

"Once." He assumed the usual Sad Little Boy expression. "But it didn't work out. *She* wanted security."

"Oh—poor woman."

"I suppose my life, in some ways, has been wasted." Repeating the lines, groping for the next ones, he could not remember the exact sequence. His mind suddenly went blank. "I had studied, you see . . . and I had hoped . . . to specialize . . ."

"Really? What specialty?" she asked.

"Pathology." He stared into his drink. He frowned at the melting ice cube. "I have a little son, you see, and I wanted to make him proud of me . . ." Jerking his head up, staring in desperation at her, he knew that these were not the proper lines. They were not the ones he had always used, and they sounded hollow, mawkish, and untrue. He had not really cared about the kid, and he had failed him, failed him abysmally.

"Oh, you have a son? Tell me all about him . . ."

Like a porcelain mannequin, smile fixed, she was sitting there in a vacuum.

"Oh, I see him very little, actually. May I get you another piece of ice? Another shrimp, Amy?"

Their dinner arrived.

Victor rolled the table in and lit the tall white candles. Victor had outdone himself. It was a splendid spectacle. The soft light flickered on polished silver, handsome china. Specks of pepper floated on the salad dressing. The wine shone ruby red, and the champagne lay in the silver bucket. Victor poured the wine, then withdrew on catlike feet.

"Oh, I didn't realize it was dinner . . ." she fluttered.

"I thought I'd surprise you."

He placed her chair for her, and they consumed the food, the elegant creations that Victor had brought. Her knee brushed his. The candles burned. The music whispered sensually, unobtrusively. She talked of Paris and her life at Vassar. She talked of Spain. She told him anecdotes without much point about her childhood in Scarsdale. And she laughed more and more feverishly. Everything was still as death, the phone did not ring, no one knocked at the door, and he could see her looking at him with quizzical expectancy.

"You are so charming . . ." He took the small white hand and kneaded it. She caught her breath. Her dark eyes melted into his.

He took her in his arms, trying to feel something. He murmured all the old mechanical phrases, pressing her lips. And she yielded willingly, with sighs. Her skin was very soft and delicate and white. It was white as cream. And somehow, somewhere, in the darkness, with just the stars, away from these candles, away from the shrouded ghost of that examining table, he could find escape—from this doomed voyage and from all the evil encompassing him.

He could get his strength back. He could fight. His luck would hold.

"I love you . . ." His voice trembled.

"Yes . . . poor boy . . ." She stroked his neck.

He lay beside her, in the cabin—as he had once lain with Maida, on a dusty coverlet, in a sepulcher.

And finally he said, "I'm sorry . . ." and turned over on his face.

"That's perfectly all right," she said in cool ladylike tones —and finally he heard her getting up.

Her high heels clicked across the linoleum, moving toward the waiting room. "Amy!" he called hoarsely. But his good-luck charm went quietly out the door, and shut it with a click.

He lay there, listening to the music playing and the records dropping in the empty rooms, watching the candle shadows dance across the ceiling. Bitch, he tried to call her, bitch. A phony, with a phony for a husband. But at last he dragged himself to his feet and snapped the record player off, and blew out the candles. He snapped on the lights and stood there, blinking, listening, in the sudden glare. He walked to the port-hole, wrenched it open.

The stars still danced on a pitch-black sea. No lights were yet visible. But they would reach Le Havre by one this morn-ing. With the fresh warm breeze blowing over his face, he reconsidered Le Havre . . . beautiful, tempting Le Havre, as the next most natural place to go. Every instinct was pushing him toward escape. He had thought about it, dreamed of it for days. The moment the ship touched France, just to run . . . run like hell across that floodlit wharf and hide in those dark alleys. How he longed to. And how sensible it sounded. With a little derring-do he could manage it, simply disappear—and when the Columbia sailed on to England tomorrow morning, he'd be far away.

He pressed his forehead against the porthole sill. His eyelids drooped. He sagged with exhaustion.

How tempting . . . for a man who hadn't put in the week he had, and had held out, clung to the illusion that silence and nonchalance were best. If he ran now, every good thing he had done, every drop of patience, self-control would be wasted. They *knew nothing*. They could not. But if he ran before the ship arrived in England, it would be tantamount to a confession of his guilt. Only a murderer would flee. So ran his thinking—and so perhaps ran theirs.

Flight was just exactly what they were hoping he would attempt. All this brainwashing, this cold war of nerves had just been leading up to it—to watching him run.

Numbly he turned back to the room, staring blindly at the half-burned candles, the grease on the plates, the champagne bucket, and the bits of shrimp lying on the floor. Then he stumbled back into his bedroom again, snapped off the lights, and threw himself down across the bed.

Fourteen more hours remained—half a night and half a day. Still he must resist them. Hold out. Keep strong. Not succumb to violence—as he had almost succumbed last night, and half a dozen times before. And if he was to do it, he must sleep. "Sleep is nature's best remedy, dear." He could hear his mother saying that when he was a little boy. "Go to sleep and face tomorrow when it comes, sonny . . ."

His eyes grew heavy. He squeezed them tight. His ears kept listening for the phone to ring. When he felt the drowsiness beginning to overcome him, he got up and set the alarm clock for midnight. That would give him one hour to decide about Le Havre definitely.

He lay back.

The ship moved on across a glittering sea.

20

∾

"VERNON...VERNON..."

Bending over him in the dark was a woman, and a woman's voice was softly saying his name. Swimming up from the depths of sleep, he smelled a sweet spicy odor, and a woman's hands were moving over him, a woman's lips were pressing his.

Then, with a yell, he was on his feet and saying hoarsely, "Get the hell out of here, you bitch, you . . ." He was snapping on the lights.

"Vernon . . ."

With the short green dress hanging off one shoulder, Ellen Stewart was sitting on the edge of his bed, hair tousled, eyes looking up at him pleadingly.

"How the hell did you get in?" He was sure he had locked the door.

"Please?" She stretched her arms toward him.

"What the hell do you want?"

"I *love* you. I . . . um . . . couldn't find you," she faltered in a plaintive voice. She rose, with sad reproach in her eyes. "You broke your promise."

She was dressed, this evening, with elaborate care. She was wearing make-up, lipstick and eyeshadow. "I love you. I had to be with you . . ." She tried to twine her arms around him again.

"Get out." He backed away. "What do you want?"

"Nothing. I . . . um . . . love you."

"Leave. I mean it."

The great eyes glowed at him. "Ever since that night in my cabin," she whispered softly, "I have loved you—wanted you. I have . . . um . . . *tried* to hide it. I have tried to resist. But tonight, when you didn't come to the captain's dinner, it was . . . um . . . um . . . like the end of the world. I *had* to find you."

He stood trapped between her and the porthole, and the pitch-black sea rushed by. The stars looked in. The alarm clock ticked on the bureau.

"Please don't be . . . um . . . angry, Vernon."

She left his side and disappeared into the examining room beyond. He heard her striking a match. Then she returned, snapping off the light in his bedroom, and she had lit one of the white candles. Its light played over her features and the masses of auburn hair. In that instant she was ravishing.

"Do you remember that night in the cabin, Vernon?" Shielding the candle with her palm until its flame grew brighter, she set it down on the bureau and sat down on the bed. "I have never forgotten it. You were . . . um . . . *so* sweet to me that night. You gave me that lollipop. You were *so* sweet and gentle . . ."

"Who sent you here? Miss Ludlow?" he asked.

She ignored his question. She smiled with tender reminiscence, and continued speaking in the soft, phony Southern voice. "My life was really miserable, Vernon. I wanted to die. I wanted to commit suicide. And then I came aboard this ship . . . and saw you."

She raised the gentle eyes to him, and color flooded her

face. "It was *so* strange. So mysterious. I thought that I was dead inside . . . I couldn't *help* loving you. You were so—so *decent* under all that bravado." Her voice shook, and she lowered it. She stared at the carpet. "And you were so very scared."

"Who's writing your lines for you?" he said. "Miss Ludlow? They're corny. You can tell her that."

"I don't know what you're talking about, Vernon." She turned her head and passed her hand over her face. "Why are you so—so—difficult?"

"Difficult!"

She rose. "I *know* that you are tired. I *know* that you are exhausted and worn out and tense." She came toward him again, gesturing, tossing back her hair. "But I also know that you are lonely—and afraid. And I want to help you."

"How? That's great," he shouted.

But she was touching him, trying to touch his cheek. "Could you love me? Just a little, Vernon? Could you?"

"You're a liar, Ellen . . ." he gasped.

"No. I've never loved anyone before, and if you . . . if you could care for me a little," she said, "I'd run away with you. I'd elope with you. I'd do something very crazy," she said.

And then she kissed him full on the mouth.

The kiss was warm and passionate—and very real. Last night he had kissed these lips, and they had been slack, completely unresponsive. But now, urgently, they were seeking his own. She was clinging to him, trying to arouse him, kissing him again. And such was chemistry that in spite of himself, he was feeling some idiot surge of desire. He had felt nothing with Amy Harrison. But with this red-headed bitch, this cheap, rotten little actress, yes. He felt a flame, a dangerous, sick, disgusting weakness—like the weakness he had once felt for Maida Jennings.

"Get out of here," he shouted, staggering back against the wall.

"Oh, Vernon, Vernon, don't be mean to me. Don't hate me. You love me. Would you marry me?" she said.

"Marry you?" He started laughing bitterly.

She fingered a brass button on his coat. "Yes," she said in a low voice. "If we were married, we could help each other. I could help you. You could help me . . ." She raised her eyes again to his, and for an instant, just an instant, he had the feeling of sincerity, something deep and very desperate that he had not seen in her before. She moved closer to him, held his eyes with hers in an unflinching steady gaze.

And even at that moment, just beyond the porthole, he heard a faint cry, a shrill squeal, and something white flew past in the darkness. The sound was repeated, and then repeated once more. Against the stars, he saw the flash of silvery wings, and then they swooped from sight.

The first gull. They must be nearing France.

"Wait a minute," he said. "Just one minute, Ellen."

He walked away from her into the darkness of his examining room. He fumbled in a couple of drawers, and then walked back into the candlelit cabin. She had moved to the bureau. By the candle's flickering light she was standing before the mirror, combing her hair with his comb. Her face turned eagerly. Her eyes shone like emeralds. He took a deep harsh breath.

"Okay, Ellen," he said. And he laid the blank check down on the bureau. "I think I understand your problem now. Shall we start talking sense?"

"What's this for?" She stared down at the check and then looked up at him. The shadows made her eyes look even brighter.

"I'm prepared to match what they are paying you," he said. "Though I'm not a rich man." He sat down on the bed. "I have only my savings, and an insurance policy made out to my son. But I could pay you a little each week out of my salary, too, as well." He was speaking breathlessly now, his eyes fixed on her changes of expression. "In return for that, all I'm asking you is the answer to a couple of questions. Okay? Agreed? You don't have to tell *them*—and you could double what you're getting."

"I don't understand you . . ." she gasped. And in the past few moments her color had changed from pink to white, and her lashes were fluttering against her cheek.

"Just tell me *what* they know, and how they know it, that's all." He walked over to her now.

"What who knows? Who's *they*?"

"Come *on*," he said.

"I don't know what you mean." She blinked her eyes. She stared at him emptily.

"Miss Ludlow, Miss Josephine Ludlow. Mr. O'Connor. Mr. Aziz . . ."

"What are you talking about?" she cried.

Then she began laughing hysterically. She seemed to go all to pieces at once. "Money? You're talking about things like *money*? People like Mr. Aziz. . . ?" She reached for the check. She tossed it in the air. "I was talking to you about *love*—and *marriage*. You're a strange man, Vernon Grove. Don't you *feel* anything? Don't you care about anything? I came here to *help* you."

"And you *can*. Stop acting."

"Acting?" She laughed bitterly.

"That's what you've been doing," he said. "You've been paid for all of this. You have no stake in this. And all I want from you, Ellen, is—is *nothing* to a girl like you . . . so what the hell is possessing you?"

She looked at him a second more. Then her eyes flared. And he knew, in that split-second, that he had used the wrong word.

"*She* is," she whispered softly.

"Who? That Ludlow woman?"

Again she laughed, feverishly. "How little you know, Vernon Grove," she said. "How childish you are . . . I didn't *tell* you about that . . . um . . . dream I had last night, did I? That dream that frightened me?"

"Oh, for God's sake, lay off that nonsense!"

She gazed at the candles. "I was in that castle. I was going up that staircase. I was in a bedroom. It was dark and huge, with a gilt mirror on the wall . . ."

The phone in the office began ringing suddenly.

She paused. She turned her head and listened to it, frowning.

"Go on," he said.

"Are you interested?" She turned to him with the wide-eyed look. "It . . . um . . . um . . . *matters?*"

"Go on, Ellen." He advanced a step.

But she waited till the phone stopped ringing. Then she turned to the candles. "Well, at first it was . . . um . . . beautiful. There were two people . . . in the bed . . . and they were happy. The *girl* was. *She* was. You know, the one in my cabin was. The spirit I've been seeing?"

"Yes, yes," he said, clenching his fingers into his palms. "Go on."

"I could . . . um . . . experience her every emotion. I

embraced him and his touch was warm. I soared like a bird, Vernon." She closed her eyes, dreamily. "I floated down a sweet dark river. I was bathed in a . . . um . . . golden ambience . . ."

"Yes, yes. Get to the point, for God's sake. And did you see this man?"

"No . . . oo . . ." She drew it out. She shook her head. "Only . . . as a shadow in the mirror . . . after he had left the bed. But he was tall, and he was wearing a raincoat." She turned her blank eyes to him.

"A raincoat."

"She didn't want him to leave. And I could feel the coldness. She pleaded with him, and got down on her knees, but he picked up his tie, and put on his raincoat, and then—and *then* . . ." With a cry she put her hands up to her face. "Oh, it was horrible."

"What was? *What* was?" His hand was gripping her arm.

"Him! He killed her. He just struck her down, Vernon. And *I* could feel it, I could feel the blow . . . um . . . cruel, searing. Then he ran away and *left* her there." Her eyes, the terrible green eyes, were staring past him now, staring beyond him.

"That's a lie." He shook her violently. "Who told you this?"

"Who *told* me? I dreamed it."

"You did not."

"I *did*, Vernon. Please. You're hurting me." She shook herself loose and ran into the office.

"Ellen!" He caught her, spun her round . . . and something crashed. "You are not leaving this room. You are telling me the truth. Who told you this? Who *saw* this thing?"

Her eyes met his with horror, she was trembling, but she said, "No one. I dreamed it."

"Who? *Who?*"

"Why? *Why*, Vernon?" she wailed, head bobbing back and forth.

"I'm asking you for the last time, Ellen . . . who told you?"

She was gasping, sobbing. "She!" she cried. "The blond woman . . . the . . . the girl in my cabin. *SHE!*"

There came a sharp rap at the door. The door burst open. And from the streaming light of the corridor, Mrs. Levy's figure walked in.

"Dr. Grove? Are you there?" she called. Then the lights went on. "*Well*, Doctor!" she said crisply. And she straightened her cap and reddened.

Ellen glided out.

"I've phoned you," Mrs. Levy said. "I paged you all over the ship just now. I'm terribly sorry to intrude on your dinner guests, but there's a woman having a *baby* down in Tourist. May I get your bag, Doctor? What else will you need?"

21

THE COLUMBIA continued to speed toward the dark jagged coastline of northern France. Lit up like a huge wedding cake, her decks atinkle with music and revelry, she swept into the starlit channel. The lights of foreign flasher-buoys began to wink across her path, and the dull bong of harbor bells began to mingle with the sound of dance music. Her motion became measured and stately.

The French tugs took over now, prodding her up the long harbor, leading her to her floodlit berth in Le Havre, and to those watching on deck, the lights twinkling along the shores, the presence of the dark low-lying coast seemed magical. This stopover in Normandy, this first landfall, always made at night, was always a great thrill for the passengers, far more glamorous than the next day's midafternoon arrival in South-ampton. Having crossed a mighty ocean, having spent nearly a week at sea, they were crowding the rails, pouring from the bars and lounges, half drunk, spellbound by every sign of approaching civilization: the squadrons of squealing gulls, the dim-lit French fishing smacks, the closer, fishier air of land.

At one fifteen precisely, the Columbia came to a stand-still.

Her engines ceased to throb. Chains clanked. Voices shouted. Alive for so many days with the sounds of move-ment, of vibration, the creaks and clatterings of wood and steel, the ship's great heartbeat now was still. The sound of human voices became sharper, more noticeable.

Down in his tiny hospital bay, in the depths of the ship, Dr. Grove sat in a chair in his white starched coat, with his white starched face. In the bed before him lay Elizabeth Organy, moaning softly. His two nurses hovered. The electric clock whirred on the wall.

His mind refused to attach itself to all these things. Numb, stunned, it was still back there in that candlelit cabin with Ellen Stewart. He sat there like a worm which has been crushed but which is still forced to remain alive. Her final words rang in his ears, their cruelty, their fantastic accuracy.

There had been an eyewitness in that castle, in that bedroom. Some human pair of eyes, which had watched, peered from the shadows (from the wardrobe? from the hallway?) and some human pair of ears, which had listened. There had been a Peeping Tom—but who? Josephine Ludlow? One of his tablemates? The press had accounted for Miss Ludlow's whereabouts: she had been in Manchester on that fatal evening. Who? Miss Ludlow had been Maida's friend—*and the eyewitness in that house had watched him go. This person had not touched the body, or reported the crime. For two years . . .* This person had stolen away, and left Maida there to decompose, with her bright dead eyes, in that cold empty house for nearly a week, until her body was accidentally discovered.

Who could have had such stoicism? Who could be so fiendish? Ellen had refused to tell him . . . but she would. Before this voyage was done.

Another hour passed. The telephone sounded. A quiet buzz.

"Dr. Grove? Paul Schultz." Schultz was a junior officer,

Mr. Anderson's assistant. "How's it going?"

"Still waiting."

"What are the prospects? The chief would like to know, Doctor."

"Who knows?" he muttered, glancing at the bed. "Maybe an hour. Maybe two. I'll let you know when it's over."

"She's supposed to be getting off in Le Havre," Schultz said. "And Anderson would *like* to get her off, if possible, before sailing time. That's at nine in the morning."

"I know when we sail," Dr. Grove replied.

"So if it looks like it's going to be any longer than two or three hours, please arrange to have her taken to a hospital in Le Havre. Let her have it there. Okay?"

"Yes," snapped Vernon Grove. "Of course. I was going to call them anyway. She'll have to go the hospital *after* it's born. But *I* can handle this."

"Okay, I'm just telling you what the chief told me to tell you."

Dr. Grove jammed down the receiver, then jiggled it until he got the ship's switchboard. "How soon will we be hooked up to shore?" he asked.

"We are hooked up," the operator answered.

"Then connect me with the hospital in Le Havre, please. Dr. Monet, the administrator."

Glancing at the woman again, listening to her rhythmic groans, he heard the phone in Le Havre buzzing and a French voice answer: *"L'hospitale generale . . . Bon jour."*

Dr. Monet spoke excellent English.

He and Vernon Grove had never met in the past eight years, but occasionally sick people from the *Columbia* had had to be removed in Le Havre and placed under his care. He was cooperative, efficient.

"Dr. Monet? This is Grove—from the *Columbia.*"

"Ah, Docteur Grove. Good morning. What can I do for you?"

"I have a woman in advanced labor . . ."

Monet sounded slightly drowsy, but he soon assured Vernon Grove that he would stand by—for any contingency. They had only to notify him and an ambulance would start for the docks at once. Meanwhile he would reserve a bed, a bassinet in the nursery.

"Thank you, Doctor."

"*De rien.* My pleasure," said Monet politely.

But by three o'clock he was not so sure it was going to be as routine as he'd thought.

Mrs. Organy's pains had slackened.

Her moans were irregular, more like sighs than moans. And the infant had not moved a fraction. Elizabeth Organy lay there, half asleep, with her eyelids drooping over dull blue eyes.

He stood above her bed, staring down at her in disbelief, at the inert form in the angel robe, his mind beginning to reel with confusion—and frustration. A smoldering rage had taken the place of his shock and numbness of two hours ago, and in this helpless creature he saw one more stroke of fate against him, one more lucky thing on Maida's side. He must dispose of this case, dispatch this woman at once to the hospital. He must be free—to find that heartless green-eyed bitch again, that little monster, and wrench the truth from her, in some dark corner of the ship, where nothing could protect her from him. Nothing interrupt.

As he moved toward the phone, it rang.

It was Schultz. Of course it was Schultz. "How's she doing?

Is it born yet? The chief would . . ."

"No . . . it isn't born," he growled. "I'm about to call the hospital now."

"Good," Schultz said. "Will you hold on for a minute? The chief would like to talk to you . . ."

In the interim that it took for Anderson to pick up the phone, a piercing scream came from the bed.

Elizabeth Organy was still screaming, with a high-pitched, eerie, oscillating sound, when Anderson's voice came on.

"You're sending her to the hospital?" rumbled the voice, then stopped. "What's that?"

"I've changed my mind, sir," Vernon Grove said hastily. "Will you excuse me?" He ran to the bed.

It was not so routine.

He had not delivered a baby in eight years. None had ever been born on the *Columbia*. He hadn't handled a complicated birth since his intern days, and then some hospital specialist had been standing right over him; there had been a blood bank, blood donors, superb equipment, trained technicians. He sent Mrs. Levy upstairs for a book on obstetrics. He thumbed through its pages. He got the woman on her feet, he walked her around and around the room, till she was sobbing, stumbling, refusing to go further.

The minutes ticked by. The hours passed. It was four o'clock, then five, five thirty. She was back on the bed again, cursing him, screaming at intervals, sitting up and clutching the sides of the bed, with her damp brown hair plastered against her pale wet cheeks, screaming and cursing him in her strange foreign tongue, unrecognizable as the timid creature in the flowered housecoat who had greeted him so humbly centuries ago.

"Oh, Doctor, can't we *do* something?" Miss Simmons kept saying.

The phone kept ringing from the bridge.

He had stopped answering it. He let Mrs. Levy answer it. Each time she answered it her voice was graver, and her eyes more accusatory as she turned them on him. But Elizabeth Organy couldn't die. Neither could her baby. He was a *doctor*, and a damned good one too. And he had always done his best, and he would. He rolled his sleeves up, scrubbed his hands, checked over his instruments, prepared for a Caesarean.

But if he operated, she could not be moved by sailing time. She would have to go on to Southampton. He would never get away. Ellen would go—free as air.

It was morning now—and disembarkation time. Outside in the corridors he could hear feet trampling, suitcases being dragged. People were going up to Quarantine. They would soon be going down the gangplanks. It was seven o'clock—but suddenly, as though by a miracle, right on the delivery table, everything was going right.

"Come *on*, Elizabeth. Bear *down*, honey..."

Miss Simmons put the cone over her nose. And it was a boy, a fat one, eight and three quarter pounds.

At seven fifteen Vernon Grove was holding him upside down and slapping his bottom.

"Thank God!" Miss Simmons began blubbering.

"Pull yourself together, Elsie. And you can phone Le Havre, Mrs. Levy..."

"But is *she* okay enough...?"

She *was*. He'd risk it. He would have to risk it. He had won the contest, and Ellen Stewart had lost. In his clouded, exhausted mind that was all that really mattered now. He was not by nature cruel or careless—or a murderer. But she had driven him beyond belief. All his hatred was focused on her now, and she must pay. She would.

The first warning whistle was blowing when the ambulance at last appeared. The exhausted woman was bundled on a stretcher, and her child was placed in a sterile bassinet. "Good girl." He patted her, and she opened her eyes for a second and smiled at him feebly. "Are the kids okay?" He remembered to ask somebody. Yes, some neighbor in Tourist, said Mrs. Levy, who was still looking at him stonily, was taking care of them, seeing that they met their father, who was meeting his family below on the wharf.

"Well, fine." He rubbed his hands together, peeled off his long white coat. The final warning whistle was blasting.

"Nice going." Schultz whistled. "Wow! Congratulations, Doctor."

"Thanks a lot," snapped Vernon Grove.

He could feel the ship moving under him as he ran up companionway after companionway, seeking her first on deck, a swift survey of the remaining passengers standing along the rails, waving goodbye to Le Havre in the morning light. The spires of the city, the yellow customs shed, the pier on which the wharf was casting long shadows were already retreating. Two French gendarmes, beside their motorcycles, were blowing kisses to somebody high on the top deck—the twin blondes.

She was not on deck, nor in any of the public rooms. He began to walk rapidly. He returned briefly to his quarters, but it was merely to shave the blond stubble from his face, and change his shirt.

He no longer felt tired. He felt an icy calm, a glassy detachment. He was watching a man called Vernon Grove from a great distance, a man whose mission was correct and justified. The walls had no dimension as he walked down them, and all sounds were far away. The ship, the sounds of the wind and the ocean barely existed now.

He passed the children's playroom, locked and silent.

He approached the cul-de-sac on silent feet.

The door of Cabin B54 was slightly ajar.

As though she had been expecting him, was waiting for him, waiting to play another of her fiendish tricks on him, the edges of the door were outlined in dim gray light. The cracks widened and narrowed. The door creaked softly, half opened, half closed rhythmically with the motion of the ship.

He paused, listening.

A cold draught licked around his feet.

Suddenly the door burst open, banging back.

And he saw that the room was empty.

The beds were stripped.

Cold gray light, chilly light, streaming through the open porthole, lay on the dingy furniture, the bare mattresses, the brown-striped ticking of the twin beds. Ellen's bed. Miss Ludlow's bed. Maida's bed.

The closet was empty.

Sodden towels lay on the floor of the bathroom, and clicking hangers swung from their steel pole.

"You looking for the ladies, Doc?" Albert the room steward had ambled in behind him. "They *gone*."

22

"G O T O F F in Le Havre," Albert said. "About an hour ago. The old lady took sick in the night, so the young girl, she changed the reservations. She said something about putting her in a hospital." He started pushing a carpet sweeper back and forth. "Ask my opinion," he said, "that old woman was dying on her feet the minute she boarded. Looked like death warmed over. And out of her head. *Was* she! Know what she kept saying over and over in this room—all by herself?"

"What?"

Albert leaned on the carpet sweeper and rolled up his eyes. Chuckling, he imitated a low and hollow tone. "Homeo, homeo, wherefore art thou, Homeo," he intoned. "You ever hear of such a mess?"

"You mean Romeo, Romeo," Vernon Grove murmured mechanically.

"*Homeo*. That's what *she* call it."

Vernon Grove left Cabin B54. Vacantly he walked away down the gray steel hall.

He started running. He searched again all over the great ship for her, as though he still expected to find her.

But he encountered no one but Aziz, who smirked at him inanely, giggled, "Iss going to rain, I theenk?" and scurried onward.

Gone!

But of course she had gone. She had known he was going to kill her. She had finished her job, and had left it to these lesser types to clean up the mess. She had fled with Josephine Ludlow, her protector, her control.

He found himself far astern, looking down at the white maelstrom of the wake, an avenue of green and white marble stretching aft through choppy water, a cataract, a witch's caldron.

The sky was clouding, turning gray. Le Havre was almost out of sight, a toy village, a diminishing steel engraving.

He stared down at the wake, and calculated his chances.

"Whatcha doing, Doc? Hey—*Doctor!*" shouted a male voice from above. Major Ewing, in cap and raincoat, was clambering down toward him, down an iron companionway.

He fled below.

He reached his quarters. Locking the door, he threw some things into a bag, added his passport, took his money out of the safe. He must hide. He must escape arrest. There were a hundred places that were safe. In some empty cabin in Tourist, in some broom closet, in the crew's dormitory, under the bunks—in the steaming, rat-ridden hold, where the passenger's cars were chained and the wooden crates lashed, he could hide during the two or three hours that it took to cross the channel. In Southampton he could sneak off the ship . . . somehow . . . wait until dark.

It was now eleven fifteen. He would have to get out of here unseen—slip below, without anyone's noticing him or guessing his purpose. It would require some circumspection, some caution. But once hidden, they wouldn't miss him, not today. Today there was no morning inspection, and his office would be closed. There was only Quarantine . . . but the hell with that.

Stuffing the wallet and passport into his breast pocket, he snapped shut the bag. With a last glance around these quarters, which had once meant security—and hell—he tiptoed toward the door. He froze. Heavy footsteps were approaching his cabin.

The footsteps paused outside. A brisk rap sounded. "Grove?" The bass voice was Anderson's.

Quick as a fox, he thrust the bag into a closet. "Yes, sir." Squaring his shoulders, he opened the door.

Anderson strode in.

Anderson sat down.

A man of few preliminaries, Anderson said, "I have a few things I'd like to discuss with you, Doctor."

And he had never had a living chance.

Anderson began by thanking him—for the baby. "You handled it well," he grunted. But his face was stern. A huge man, monolithic in his braided uniform, with a glum woodcarving of a face, he stared at the wall. "I hope we didn't botch it." He squinted steely eyes. "Was she okay in your opinion? And the child? It was safe to move them?"

"Yes, sir," he said.

Anderson's huge hairy hand with its plain gold wedding band lay across the knife crease in his dark blue trousers. "They were poor people," he said. "Her husband was meeting her." He smoothed the crease. "Did she arrive at the hospital in good shape? You checked their condition?"

"Yes, certainly," he lied. "Surely. She'll be just fine, Mr. Anderson."

Anderson's eyes bored into him. It was like standing before

the Judgment Seat. "Been a pretty rough trip for you, hasn't it, Grove?" he asked, not without kindliness.

"Yes, rather, sir."

Anderson cleared his throat. "That's another point I want to discuss with you," he said. "Brightwood has applied for a reinstatement."

"*Brightwood . . . Sir?*"

"He phoned us in Le Havre today." Anderson picked up a paper clip lying on the doctor's desk. "He seems to think that somebody pulled a fast one on him, in New York. He got drunk in some tavern with some woman, Tuesday evening, and didn't come to till the ship had pulled out." He had bent the clip into a single straight line. He laid it on the desk. "He's willing to fly over now, pick us up in Southampton. What's your opinion?"

"Mine?"

Anderson nodded. He got up and moved over to a port-hole. The leaden sea slid past—and a gull, with legs tucked under it, trying to keep pace with the ship. And the green tip of the first of the Channel Islands.

"I'm not inclined to excuse him," Anderson mused, still staring out over the water. "But hell, good doctors aren't easy to come by, and I haven't lined up anybody yet in England." He turned round. "You deserve a rest, Doctor."

"Yes, sir."

But he was staring at Anderson's face. Didn't the chief know? Had it all been utterly sub rosa? Jenkins and Doyle had dared to cooperate without the knowledge of the chief exec?

It appeared that way.

Yes. Anderson was smiling at him, as much as Anderson ever smiled, a crack of tolerant sympathy.

"So if you'd like, I'll cable him, and you can damn well see that he does double duty on the westbound crossing. Okay, Grove?"

"Okay, sir. Yes. It's your decision. Certainly."

"Fine." Anderson grunted and walked toward the door. "Well, at least he seems to have the sea in his blood . . . just like you and me." He grinned. "So long, Grove." He stuck the huge hand out. "Take it easy today." His eyes twinkled. "Well, I got a ship to land." And he went striding off erectly down the corridor.

Seeing the broad back vanish, Vernon Grove felt a lump come into his throat. Anderson had been the only man he had ever admired. Anderson had been the only father he had ever known. But it was too late for sentiment. Waiting only until the heavy footsteps had ceased their echoing, he took the bag from the closet again and closed the door of his quarters behind him.

He tiptoed rapidly around corners to the elevator. No use bothering with unlocking all the gates between the classes. They were still locked, and would be till Southampton, and each gate would mean a delay of several seconds. The elevator would drop him instantly to the engine room or the hold. He pressed the Down button, eyes glued to the lighted indicator.

The car was still up on the bridge deck. Probably Anderson had just stepped out of it. But soon it began its descent, dropping without pause from deck to deck. And the door slid open.

"Here he is!"

Out stepped O'Connor and Aziz, grinning.

He started to bolt into the elevator, and O'Connor lunged in after him, pressed the Hold button, and Aziz scurried in too. "Oh no you don't, Doctor. No, you don't." O'Connor's grip was like iron, his laughter gargantuan.

The doors of the elevator closed.

"What the hell is this?"

"We've been delegated . . ." O'Connor brayed. Aziz exploded into giggles.

"Delegated—by whom?" he asked.

"You'll see." O'Connor gripped him tightly.

The elevator moved upward to Main. It stopped. They hustled him out. Aziz squeezed his arm fiercely. "There's been some mistake," he kept assuring them. The main lobby was full of people. Jenkins scooted past. "Got him?" he snickered. They dragged him toward the lounge.

"What is this? Lay off!" He was sped inside—past onyx tables, leaning gilt pillars, and Harry smiling cryptically behind the bar. They led him up to a corner table, where the Ewings were. And the major whooped with glee and leaped to his feet.

"You got him? Great, Father. Good work, fellas. Nicely done."

"It was quite a scrimmage, but we made it," O'Connor said.

"Foughts like *ti*-ger," Aziz panted.

"Oh, the poor *dear*," Judy Ewing cooed. "He looks positively *scared*. Here, sit down and take a load off your feet, Doctor. By me. Aren't they the silliest?"

"What is this?" he asked again in a small voice.

"Why, just a little celebration. A farewell party," she said. "For *you*. We couldn't leave the *Columbia* without saying goodbye. And you've been *so* elusive . . ."

23

"Y O U R H A N D is shaking like a leaf, Doctor. You look exhausted. I heard about that baby you delivered this morning . . ."

A Scotch and water was placed before him.

He did not touch it.

"*Ellen* got off in Le Havre, you know," Judy said. "Her aunt was very, very ill. They were supposed to go to Scotland. The poor child had to change the tickets, and do everything. She was just beside herself, I hear."

The room swung. It tilted. It turned upside down, so that Mrs. Ewing's dangling pearl earrings were sometimes close to him, sometimes far away. Aziz's turban was a huge white balloon. O'Connor's cassock was an inquisitor's robe.

"Have a cigarette. Oh, break down, for once."

He accepted the cigarette—his first in several years.

He drew on it deeply, and it tasted good.

But he could not accept any other miracle.

They were *not* his friends.

They were not just four old jolly pals, full of high jinks and playful spirits, people who liked him, people he would never see again.

He sat there, puffing on the cigarette, which soon made him feel nauseated, with his bag still at his feet, ready to run.

The Channel Islands slid by, and the glasses clinked. Judy Ewing kept chattering. O'Connor beamed at him benevolently. Aziz's dark eyes darted at him from behind their horn-rimmed spectacles. *One of them knew. One of them had been there* . . . in Glyn Tower, in that bedroom. And at any second they were going to tell him.

"Did you hear about Mr. Aziz's new girl?" Judy Ewing was giggling.

"No, I didn't hear about it." He took a desperate sip of Scotch.

"Well, it's *so* cute." She lowered her voice and leaned toward his sleeve. "He met her just last night. In Tourist. After the captain's dinner, which you didn't attend, and we were so disappointed." She gave a meaningful, mysterious smile.

"I'm very sorry . . ."

"It's all *right*." She touched him. "Anyway, she's Spanish. They were having a party in Tourist afterward, and Mr. Aziz went prowling, and *she* fell for him, evidently, and *he* fell for her. Like a ton of bricks. She's from Andalucía. She's even invited him to her home."

"Very nice," he said.

"What's you sayink about me, Mees Ewing?" Aziz now broke in, with a gleaming smile, from across his hot tea. "What you tellings Meestair Grove abouts me?"

"I was telling him about your *girl*, your sweetheart . . . the one who's asked you to visit her in Granada."

"Oh—*yess*." He giggled. "Thass fine. Yess. She ver' nice." He rolled his eyes eloquently.

"And are you going to Granada, Mr. Aziz?" Dr. Grove asked carefully.

"Sure. Granada? Maybe yess. Iss nawthing . . ." The dark face lit up like an ebony moon. With white teeth flashing, nodding solemnly, Aziz said, "She make ver' nice wife for me.

I *theenk*. In Spanish cowntry they like Moorish. Part Arabia. I go mebbe after tour of Shakespeare cowntry to my Desdemona."

"Omar, you are quite a card," laughed Ewing, nudging Aziz in the ribs. "Doctor, isn't he a character?"

Characters, indeed.

Or simply slightly eccentric human beings, people with ordinary human foibles, whose quirks he had mistaken for deceit and slyness? He knew that there were many other people like them; he had encountered many a grotesque, a caricature, in his day. He knew that the sea, and the intimacy of a seven-day cruise, could exaggerate and distort people's personalities. Strange illusions could arise. But he still mistrusted them. There had been too many coincidences, too many meaningful looks and glances.

They were all talking now about their plans for Europe, and reminiscing. And what jolly reminiscences they were! Perhaps there was some technicality involved. They could not clap the handcuffs on until the ship reached shore.

"Far more restful than flying," O'Connor was saying. "And I even enjoyed those rainy days. I got a great deal of work done—on that study of mine."

"What study was that, Father?"

"Oh, a rather long paper I'm supposed to deliver at the conference this week. Behavior patterns among delinquents on the Lower East Side. I do a lot of work with boys clubs."

"I see," he said, recalling the cablegram and the athletic gestures.

"And did you know the major won the ping-pong tournament?"

"No. Did you, Major?"

"Bob won everything there was to win." Judy laughed. "Except first prize in the Talent Show. He got the *best* bingo cards. People loathed him. And guess what? Last night, right after the captain's dinner, he guessed the exact mileage in the ship's pool. This has been the luckiest trip for us."

Lucky indeed.

The food had been marvelous, the service superb. They had all gained at least ten pounds apiece. And they'd met so many interesting, charming people. "But best of all, honey," the major said, in a voice choked with sentiment, "were *these* people." And he lifted his glass. "To our dear friends, members of our little family, long may they wave, we wish them every happiness. Father? Omar?"

"Hear, hear," Father O'Connor said.

"I *tea* drinker. Forbidden religion, alcohols. But I drink to you—*nize* Americans."

"And to our good ship's doctor, the best damned doctor on the entire ship."

Everybody laughed at the major's joke, none louder than the major.

"Our only regret is that we've seen so little of him," the major continued hoarsely, still on his feet. "And that a little romance we'd been keeping our eye on didn't altogether jell."

"Oh, come on, Bob. That's enough, silly." Judy Ewing tugged at her husband's sleeve.

"But it's true, honey. Didn't we keep our fingers crossed?"

"Shush, Robert."

At last they got up to go.

The Channel Islands had all gone past. The mainland of

England was in sight. The engines were slowing noticeably . . . and the final moments of this voyage had come. One by one, each rose from his chair and shook his hand, and said goodbye. And he could not possibly believe it. There was something wrong. There had to be.

"Goodbye, Doctair. I send you postcard mebbe from Shakespeare cowntry." Aziz departed with a last gleaming smile, a flash of his brown hand, like an autumn leaf.

"Thank you, Dr. Grove. And good luck, my son," O'Connor said. "And I enjoyed that story about the corn flakes." His blue eyes twinkled. "And our brief discussion of the supernatural."

"*Great* trip. Take it easy, boy." His hand was wrung by Major Robert Ewing. "Come to see us in Florida . . . drop into the condominium any time. It's modern, air-conditioned, close to the beach. Judy, give him our address, honey . . ."

Mrs. Ewing lingered on. She took out a pencil and a scrap of paper. "I don't suppose you'll ever get there, but if you ever do . . ." She scribbled a line, and then looked up with a reddening face. "Bob was silly to tease you about Ellen. It was just a schoolgirl crush, a childish infatuation. She was only nineteen, after all . . . and I didn't mean to put my two cents' worth in."

"That's okay, Mrs. Ewing."

"It would never have worked out. I think that you were wise and acted very gentlemanly. May I kiss you goodbye, Doctor? I've been wanting to—for ever so long." She stood on tiptoes and pecked his cheek, then ran off with a girlish air. "Bye!" She waved to him from the lounge's threshold, and then was gone.

"God Almighty!" Harry said. "What did you ever do to deserve *them?*"

The ship's horn was blasting her first greeting to South-ampton harbor.

He watched them standing in line at Quarantine—with all the other passengers. From a secluded corner of the upper deck, he watched them moving down the gangplank—with the crowds. Judy carried a bulging straw bag, and the major had a movie camera and golf clubs strapped across his shoulder. Aziz was bearing the large black cardboard suitcase he had used at the Talent Show. And when O'Connor appeared in vestments and black homburg, a man on the pier, in clerical garb, a man with a round cherubic face, started waving and shouting, "Tom, you old son-of-a-gun!"

"Dawkins!" O'Connor roared. And they pumped hands vigorously.

He saw Amy Harrison mincing along in her white suit, turning, as she reached the wharf, and for one moment gazing ruefully back at the *Columbia*. Then, limping toward her, came a tall handsome man with a cane. She spied him, and started running with her arms outstretched.

And now, at last, he could believe it.

The ship was totally silent, totally empty.

He kept straining his ears for sirens, but there were none.

He kept expecting Miss Ludlow and Ellen to appear with a phalanx of policemen or plainclothesmen. But the docks were bare, spattered only by the rain that was beginning to fall in large black drops.

There was nothing but the bleak, drab vista of South-ampton's familiar slopes, the brilliant flowers in her gardens, the array of chimney pots like teapots marching down to the sea. There was only Ellen—those two evil women—and the

rest of it had all been fantasy, a self-generated plot, an explanation that he had devised himself, simply because no other
logical explanation was possible. But those four other people
at his table had not known, Anderson could not have known,
Jenkins, Doyle could not have known . . . and perhaps not
even Brightwood. And very obviously, not the police. Only
those two women.

Why?

Why had they done it? Why had they fled?

Staring at Southampton, staring around at the empty
decks, he felt a cold chill creeping up his spine once more.

He wasn't free of *them.*

Somewhere in the world they existed, and they knew his
secret, and as long as they knew it he wasn't free. They could
blackmail him, they could come aboard the ship again, they
could make him dance to the same old tune . . . and never,
never in his life would he ever be free of the evil eyes, the
grisly smile of Maida Jennings.

He *must* be free. It wasn't madness now . . . like this morning, or last night, when she had kissed him as Maida had, or
that night in the fog when she had hovered around the win-
dowpane. He must find her, and know for sure who that eyewitness was . . . stamp the supernatural out forever. *There had
been an eyewitness.* ESP was a fake, a vicious fake. And he
must prove it to himself forever.

He started walking down to his cabin. He must start research. He must start looking for her. He must track her to
the ends of earth.

A bellhop stopped him at the foot of a companionway.
"Dr. Grove, I was asked to give this letter to you when we
reached Southampton, and not before. The young lady spe-
cified it when she left this morning."

The handwriting on the envelope was Ellen's, and the instructions were plain: NOT TO BE DELIVERED UNTIL ARRIVAL SOUTHAMPTON.

"Thank you," he said.

He waited till the man had disappeared. He braced himself against the wall. But it was only a couple of carefully inscribed lines.

Dearest Vernon, Aunt Victoria is ill, and I must leave immediately. But I shall try to phone you when your ship reaches England. I know you are the man in the raincoat, but it doesn't seem to matter. Love. E.S.

24

NO ONE was in his quarters. They were darkened by the rain. He sat down at his desk and phoned the switchboard.

"Are we connected to shore yet?" he asked. And she said yes, they had been for the past half hour.

"Have there been any calls from France for me?"

France? No, she answered. But he'd had two already from London. She'd been trying to locate him.

"London? Who in London?"

"She wouldn't give me her name, but she started calling you the minute we were hooked up," said the operator. "Are you going to be there awhile? She's probably going to try again."

"Yes," he said.

He sat there, tearing bits of the desk blotter off. Anderson's paper clip still lay where he had left it, and he picked it up and tried to bend it back to its original shape. The rain slashed against the windowpanes, and the boat-train whistle shrieked. He heard the sound of the train starting, disappearing into the distance.

The phone rang.

"Ready with London," said the operator's voice. "Just a minute, please. Go ahead, London."

"Hello, Vernon. Is that you?" Her voice was very brisk, and very bright.

"Yes, where are you, Ellen?"

"I'm in *London*," she said gaily. "I've been calling you and calling you. Didn't anybody give you my message?"

"No." He loathed the brittle tone of her voice. "How did you get there? Where *are* you?"

"I flew across the channel," she replied. "I left poor Aunt Victoria in the Le Havre general hospital. There was nothing I could do for her, so I just flew over here—to be with you. Are you coming up?" she asked. "Can you leave the ship? Or shall I come to *you*?"

"No . . . don't come here," he said. "I'll—get up to London. Where *are* you?"

"You don't sound too happy about it," she said.

"Yes. Yes, I'm *delighted*, Ellen. I—"

"We talked about marriage last night. Have you forgotten?"

"No. Of course not." He couldn't stand this brash new way of speaking. She had dropped every trace of Southernism. There was not even the suggestion of a stammer. "Simply tell me where you are . . ."

"I'm all alone in the world now," she said with just a vague quaver in her voice. "I have no one to advise me."

"Yes, yes, Ellen. Where can I find you?"

"Something . . . um . . . um . . . t-terribly strange is *happening* to me, Doctor." Suddenly the old faltering, soft-voiced Ellen was back. "I'm *f-frightened!*"

"Yes, yes, yes. Just give me your *address*."

Her voice became a wail. "I don't know . . . um . . . *where* I am. I'm . . . um . . . um . . . *lost!*" It faded.

There was silence.

"*Ellen!*"

And then, from far away, as though some lost child were

calling to him from some dark lonely street, he heard her crying, "I *need* you. Oh!" With a gasp, the cry broke off, and he heard no more, just the humming of the open wire.

"Ellen! *Ellen!*"

There was a click. The connection was broken off. The dial tone came on.

He jiggled the receiver frantically. He called the ship's operator. "We were cut off just now," he said. "Can you reconnect me with that number?"

"I'll try, Doctor."

He heard her calling London, and the London operator answering, "Very sorry, madam. I will try to reconnect you." He heard the call go through, and the phone ringing at the other end. "I'm very sorry, madam, but they are not responding at the moment."

"Can you trace that call for me?" he broke in to London. "Where it was coming from, the address? I'm very anxious to locate the address."

"One moment, please, sir."

There were a lot of clicks and buzzes, faint British voices on other wires, then she came on again.

"You wish to know the address from which that call was made, sir?" she asked politely.

"Yes. It's urgent. Vital."

"I am sorry, but we are not permitted to give out that information, sir. The number came from a private home. It is unlisted. You might try through the official channels, sir. Would you wish me to connect you with the proper authorities?"

"No, thank you," he said.

He placed the receiver slowly back on its hook. He waited. He picked up the paper clip.

. . .

The rain continued to fall. The sky grew darker and more leaden. On the docks, they were unloading from the *Columbia*, taking new freight on, and from the neighboring cabins he could hear the whine of vacuum cleaners, the slam of doors, as the stewards and stewardesses moved about, preparing for the fresh load of passengers due by midnight tonight.

He picked up the phone again. "Will you connect me with the Le Havre general hospital, please? Dr. Monet, the administrator."

"Certainly, Doctor. Did they ever manage to reconnect that call?" she asked.

"No, Evelyn," he said.

"Le Havre Generale. In France?"

He heard her placing the call for him, and eventually the familiar voice of Dr. Monet came on: "Yes, Doctor, the little boy and the mother are doing excellently. The husband is also here. It's a very nice little family."

"Did you admit any other patient from the *Columbia* today," Dr. Grove was finally able to ask. "A Mrs. Victoria Graham?"

"A Mrs. Victoria Graham?"

"She may also have been admitted under the name of Josephine Ludlow," Dr. Grove said. "I didn't send her."

"Oh—Graham," said Monet. "Yes, Graham. I had to think for a moment," he said. "I had to look at my record chart. Yes. A Mrs. Graham is here. But she was admitted privately —by her niece. I did not realize she was from your ship."

"How is she?" Dr. Grove asked after a pause.

And after a pause, Monet answered gravely, "She is dead, Doctor."

"*Dead?*"

"She died almost immediately after her arrival," Monet was saying—from somewhere way, way off in France. "She had a cerebral accident. Very severe. Around eight o'clock this morning. We did a spinal, and we gave her oxygen. But it was impossible to save her life." After a pause, he asked, "You did not examine this patient on the ship, Doctor?"

"No," said Vernon Grove.

"Curious," said Monet. "There were many symptoms of arterial disease. Marked deterioration of the mind and the body. I am surprised this woman was even able to travel. I will send you a report on her, if you like."

"Thank you, Doctor. How old was she?" Vernon Grove asked.

"About seventy, I believe."

"Is her niece still there?"

"No. She had to leave, to make some sort of arrangements. She has not yet returned. A very attractive young woman, but with much difficulty with her speech. And much distraught—*naturellement.* Did you know her on board, Doctor?"

"Barely," said Vernon Grove. "She didn't happen to leave a phone number, or an address with you, Doctor? Where I could reach her, offer my condolences."

"No," said Monet. And then—"One moment. I will check to be sure." After an eternity, he repeated, "No," adding, "But I will tell her that you called, when she returns."

"Thank you very much, Dr. Monet."

"A life for a life, eh?" Monet said softly. "It was at eight o'clock, about, that we were sending you the ambulance."

Dead!
Josephine Ludlow had never been aboard the ship . . . or

she lay, a drained gray corpse, in the morgue of a French hospital, an enigma to the very end.

So that left only Ellen.

Ellen Stewart, lost in London, who had said, insisted, at the point of death, three times, that she was no more than a gently reared child, traveling with her aunt from Edinburgh, her aunt whose body was the body of a woman of seventy, and whose smile was vacant, and whose reactions were confused.

He picked up the phone again.

"Operator," he said, "this may take time, and it's going to cost a lot of money, but I'd like you to make a direct call, a direct call to a place in Virginia, called Marshall, and the family's name is Stewart, I don't know the initial, but it's Stewart."

"Transatlantic, Doctor, in other words?" she said.

"Yes, but I'm paying for it."

"Stewart," she said. "And that place was Marshall?"

"Yes." He felt the nerves in his scalp tingling.

"Do you spell Stewart with a 'u' or a 'w'?" she asked.

"S-t-e-w-a-r-t."

"Okay, Doctor. Here we go," she said. "But maybe you'd just better hang up for a while."

He didn't hang up. He sat listening to the long complicated relays and requests that ensued, and thought of the great thick cable swinging in the dark green depths of the Atlantic, hanging there beneath all those miles . . . and of the east coast of America, and of the telephone poles marching down the dusty highways, marching up into the Virginia hills. And that little village, just a crossroads. But the old red brick house, the apple orchard—*they* had never existed, they were lies.

"Richmond," said a far-off Southern voice. "Front Royal,"

said another one. "Marshall? Yayus. I will connect you with Information."

"That must be out in the country," the ship's operator commented while they waited an interminable time.

"There is an E. Stewart listed in Marshall," came the faint voice at last. "And the number is 212."

"Thank you, Front Royal. Will you ring that number for us, please?"

"That's the only Stewart listed?" he interrupted.

"Yayus."

They rang. And he sat there with bated breath.

But the distant buzzes only added up to three, and then there was a click, and a mechanical voice came on: "That number you are trying to reach has been disconnected."

"I'm so sorry, Doctor," the ship's operator said.

Disconnected because she had gone to Europe—for the summer—with Aunt Victoria? He sat there with glazed eyes. He sat there with his head down, pressed against the blotter, and the room grew ever more silent, darker, in the falling rain. The rain drizzled on the docks, and he thought of the way she had sung that song, the way her eyes had had the strange power of piercing into him. The way she had never hated him, but had always been so gentle, so very soft, and the way her voice had sounded over the phone just now—frightened, and then breaking off. But it was impossible. E. Stewart and the red house and that father and the apple trees were lies. The dead did not return. They did not take revenge.

Sharply, like some screaming woman, the phone rang in the silence.

"Is this Dr. Vernon Grove?" asked a pleasant British voice.

"Yes, it is."

"Ready with Dr. Grove, madam. Go ahead, please."

Ellen said crisply, "Thank you so much. Is that you, Vernon?"

"Yes. *Yes.* What *happened* to you?"

"I've been trying to reach you, but your line was always busy. Are you coming up to town? Can you come at once? I'm at 42 Kenilworth Terrace, and the apartment is 2B. Ring the downstairs bell and I will buzz the clicker."

"Forty-two Kenilworth Terrace, 2B." His voice shook. "Yes, Ellen."

"Come immediately," she said.

25

HE PEELED off his uniform, changed to civilian clothes, and since it was raining hard, put on his hat and raincoat. At the last minute Miss Murphy saw him, just outside the door of his waiting room. She was skipping by very briskly. "Going somewhere fun?" She cocked her freckled face. "Oh, I *hope* so. You deserve it . . . and Phil thinks so too." She hurried onward, in the usual direction.

He frowned after her vaguely, then moved on with purpose, a man with a hat and raincoat on, walking up companionways, moving out on deck, walking down a gangplank very stiffly, erectly, with his eyes staring straight ahead.

"Sailing time's at midnight, Doctor," said someone at the foot of the gangplank.

"Yes, I know." He walked on swiftly now, and out through the empty customs shed, showing his identity card to the lone man at the gate. The boat-train had long since gone, but he found a bus leaving for London in ten minutes. He got aboard it and sat in a seat by himself, near the rear, not noticing the landscape, merely jouncing, with his hands twitching in his lap.

The steam gathered on the windowpanes, and the rain increased. They were passing Glyn Tower now, probably, but he must not think about it. Glyn Tower soon would be in ruins. It was all shut up and dark now anyway, and its furniture had been sold. He had read some article in the newspapers about their turning it into a housing development. Or a girls' academy. Its evil had never existed. That was simply one of Maida's inventions, her idea of something glamorous. And he hadn't killed her. And she lay in a churchyard, moldering, in a white satin shroud.

"We're an evil lot, luv . . . Fresh blood. You're such a nice, simple, naïve American . . ."

Possession was an old wives' tale. A girl, barely twenty, had conceived of a wicked gimmick, and gone to the public library, and used her imagination . . . just to wind him around her thumb. For *no* reason. Just as Maida had.

He saw the bright dead gray eyes gazing up at him by candlelight. He saw the hazel eyes quickening. "Of course, it has a curse on it, Doctor . . ." He felt her fingers twitching along his arm. He saw her standing by a yellow sofa, in black satin lounging pajamas, brandishing her cigarette holder. "I *knew* you'd come. I *willed* it."

The bus jounced onward. The lights of London loomed in the rain. It was dusk, growing darker, and the fog and mist rose from the streets. The evening crowds jostled him. He had a long time finding a taxi.

"Forty-two Kenilworth Terrace . . ."

Glittering wet streets flew by—and darker ones. It could not be the address Maida had given him . . . but he could no longer remember that address. He tried and tried, shivering there in the mildewed cab. It moved slowly past old houses and dripping trees, into a huge old-fashioned square with a park in the middle.

All London squares looked alike, he told himself, in the rain and fog, but there was the same eerie silence here, the loneliness, the total absence of passers-by.

He paid the driver and got out. The house was one of a set of old Victorian houses, and it had a stoop, a dim-lit vestibule. There was no doorman, just a set of buzzers.

He leaned against the wall, breathing heavily.

He pressed 2B.

There was no name next to it, just an empty plate.

Profound silence ensued. Not a footfall could be heard.

He touched the buzzer again, and kept his finger on it, counting five.

At last the heavy inner door began to buzz and vibrate, and he pushed it open and walked in.

Red-carpeted stairs lay before him, and a narrow carpeted hall. The hall was lit by a chandelier with a very weak lightbulb. He heard no sound, from above or below. The house breathed quiet and respectability, an uncanny quiet.

"Ellen?" he called up the stairs.

"Ellen?" he called again.

He took a deep harsh breath and began to mount the thickly carpeted stairs.

The door of flat 2B stood slightly ajar.

Dim light seeped from the cracks, but still he could hear no sound.

"Ellen? Ellen dear? It's me. Vernon. Are you there?"

"Come in," a cool, clear voice replied.

And then he saw her, and a hoarse cry, a cry of sheer terror, rose in his throat.

She was seated in a huge dim drawing room on a yellow sofa, facing him, in black lounging pajamas. Her shoulder-length hair was burnished gold, and her skin the shade of honey. Her eyes—*gray* eyes—were staring at him, blazing at him, with a cold inhuman mockery. She was brandishing a long jeweled cigarette holder.

"Come in, luv," she said softly.

26

HE STOOD STUNNED, revolted, para-
lyzed. Behind him the door drifted shut with a faint click.
Time's dimensions had vanished. He had come full cycle. He
was looking at Maida as she had looked on an October evening long ago. She was smiling as Maida had smiled, tossing
her golden head, gesturing with the cigarette holder. "I *willed*
you to come, Vernon." Her voice was a running brook of
silver, icy cold. "I *knew* you'd get here. And you came. Isn't
that divine?"

Her movements were Maida's, graceful and sensual, as she
swayed off into the shadows of the room.

He tried his best to speak, but his tongue clove to the roof
of his mouth, as the impact of the room itself, this horrible
room began to strike his consciousness. For it was exactly like
Maida's old flat, complete in every detail—the yellow curtains, the pots of gardenias, the books, the pictures, just as he
had seen them on that rainy evening two years ago.

A gas fire hissed upon the hearth. Outside there was the
same dull patter of the falling rain. From the bedroom he
heard the same grotesquely familiar sound of a delicate chime
striking the hour of six.

As the last note ended, she turned from the shadows, and
he could see the brilliant sparkle of the emerald ring on her
hand.

"I so badly want you to see Glyn Tower, luv, and tonight we will go . . ."

In the gleam of a lamp her gray eyes flashed, and with a supreme effort of will he forced his own to meet them. "I . . ." The word rasped in his throat, garbled, lost in a rattle of phlegm.

"What were you about to say, Vernon?" She floated toward him. "That you have to get back to your ship? Was that it?" She smiled brilliantly. "You will never go back to your ship, luv. You are staying with *me*." Her voice went echoing through the labyrinths of terror, back through time. "And we shall sleep in Queen Elizabeth's room. I didn't show you the dungeons, did I? You wouldn't want to be a grand seigneur? Sir Vernon Grove, Baronet?"

Her laugh was like the sound of shattering glass. And for Vernon Grove the spell was shattered. This had to be an act, a masquerade, another trick. But it was impossible for her to know these things—impossible.

Yet she was repeating the precise words that Maida had once said to him on a dusty bed in a pitch-black bedroom in an empty house on a lonely estate—with the same inflection, the same mocking, deliberate maddening drawl.

Her voice grew harsher, more imperious. "Blackmail? Is that what you're afraid of, darling boy? You don't like to be possessed?" She was coming nearer now, with glittering eyes. "You will learn to like it, luv. I have *arranged* for you to like it, luv. It doesn't *matter* that you murdered me."

"I didn't murder her," he gasped.

"You didn't?" She smiled mockingly.

"No," he said.

"Oh, Vernon luv." Her lips were twisted with contempt. "What use is it to lie to me? *I* felt the pain and agony. I gave my *life* for you—and lay there in the darkness all alone." Her voice broke in a sob. "I *loved* you, and you left me—*hated* me."

"I didn't."

But those gray eyes were implacable. "You *killed* me, Vernon. It was cold-blooded murder."

"It wasn't. You're a lying bitch. It *wasn't.*"

He was glaring at her now, yelling hoarsely in a voice he did not recognize as his own. He was shouting in a stifling void, his words muffled by soft rugs, thick curtains. He was boiling with the rage of the years, the chains that Maida had so senselessly heaped on him.

"She brought it on herself," he yelled. "I didn't mean to do it. All I did was hit her once, and she fell, but I never meant to kill her, even though she deserved it!"

In the huge dim room there was sudden silence, so profound that he could hear his own voice reverberating into the shadows. He saw the girl in black pajamas sag and crumple. And then a tall grim figure, a man wearing a turban, glided swiftly in from the room beyond.

"Good," said Omar Aziz. "Bravo!" Aziz grinned. "Thank you, Doctair. And thank *you*, my dear. We have all we need, right here, recorded for posterity." With a triumphant flourish, he held out a cartridge of tape.

The girl was putting her hand slowly up to her hair. She sank into a chair. He saw the long red hair slide loose about her shoulders. It was Ellen.

"I'm . . . um . . . um . . . sorry, V-Vernon," she said.

Numbly he watched as she tossed the yellow wig aside and delicately slid the contact lenses from her eyes into her palm. Her eyes were green now, enormous and blue-green, and the look she gave him was one of infinite sadness, weariness.

Aziz, with the tiny tape-recording cartridge balanced in his palm, was strutting before the fireplace, white teeth gleaming in the swarthy face, spectacles glittering in the glow of the gas fire.

He turned, gesturing once more with the cartridge as one might brandish a precious gem, and in his other hand he now held a small revolver. From his lips there came a high-pitched giggle.

"Batt-el Crick? Ees Meechagan?" He laughed insanely. "What you think of me *now*, Corn Flakes Boy? You like? You think you ver' lucky man? Get away with murder?"

He moved toward Vernon Grove and peered into his face contemptuously.

"What you theenk happen to you now, Doctair? Can you look in future and tell? You have ESP, maybe?" Again the high-pitched laugh. "You go back to ship, to make fools of women again? How you like our little drama?" He gestured at the luxurious room. "Stage set fine, good lighting, *real* properties." With high glee he gloated. "And how you like the fog scene and the mad scene on *Columbia*? Ver' much like Shakespeare, don't you theenk?"

Vernon Grove said nothing.

"And this performance tonight, Doctair." Aziz was smirking exultantly. "Was it not magneeficent?" He turned to Ellen, who sat huddled in her chair. "Geev line again, Mees Stewart. 'You nevair go back to ship. You stay with *me* in Glyn Tower . . .'"

But Ellen was staring straight ahead. Her green eyes glistened moistly in the light of the gas fire.

"Go ahead, *say* line again."

She sat there motionless.

Laughing indulgently, Aziz shrugged, then flashed a gleaming smile at Vernon Grove. "How you feel now, Doctair Romeo? Frightened? No?"

"No," Vernon Grove replied.

And he wasn't. He felt some queer sense of the ridiculous—and beyond that he felt only calm, a feeling of resignation, such as inevitably must come to every man whose flight is finally ended. There was a certain relief to know at last that his pursuers were merely human, and that someone had to have been at Glyn Tower on that fatal night, a living eyewitness.

"Get coat!" Aziz growled at Ellen.

But for a moment longer she sat staring at the walls, apart, abstracted, apathetic. Then, as if transfixed, she rose and moved like a sleepwalker into the bedroom, reappearing in the light tan coat she had worn on deck the night of the storm.

Aziz handed her the cartridge.

She accepted it numbly.

"Take cab. Tell gentlemen at Yard prisoner is waiting, safe and sound. Unless . . ." The high-pitched giggle echoed through the room and broke off abruptly. When Aziz spoke again, it was in the voice of someone else, someone quite unlike the absurd student from Basra. Gone was the Middle East accent, the shrill burlesque, gone were the grotesque malapropisms. The voice had darkened, grown intense and beautifully modulated. "Unless, through some fortuitous circumstance, Dr. Grove should attempt to escape pending the arrival of the police—in which event," he smiled, "it would be my supreme pleasure to destroy him in the act of flight."

There was again a dead dull silence, broken only by the sound of Ellen's breathing and the hissing of the fire. Vernon

Grove stared at Aziz, at the turban, the dark suit, trying to see beyond the spectacles, trying to pierce that grinning mask, seeking some clue to this strange creature's identity.

For he knew now that Aziz could have no official connection with the police, and what he had done could have no official sanction. From the very start Aziz had acted on his own, obeying the dictates of a crazed mind, driven by hatred and thirsty for revenge.

"Go, Mees Stewart," he hissed now.

"No!" Ellen raised her head.

She cast a frightened look at Vernon Grove.

"No?" Aziz's voice was soft, too soft. He slithered toward her.

The absurd accent returned, the hissing intonation, but now the timbre was deeper and more menacing.

"You disobey, my leetle one? You weesh to go back to the *gutter* where I found you—sniveling for money to pay for your addiction? Go, Ellen!"

Tears began to slide down her cheeks. She clutched the cartridge tightly. She stood forlorn, her throat convulsing. "You . . . um . . . um . . . can't do this to him. He didn't really mean it." Her eyes grew huge and agonized. "He didn't really m-murder her."

"Ha! You little fool. You stupid hillbilly. How do *you* know what he did? Were you in that castle that night? Were you listening to them? *I* was. I know *exactly* what happened. And he *meant* to kill her . . . kill my Maida."

"I . . . um . . . believe him. I believe in Dr. Grove."

"Who cares what you believe? For two *years* I've waited for this, *lived* for it, and thought of nothing else. I've spent a fortune. I had to leave my poor old sister to die in Le Havre. For *this*. For this evidence. And there it is, right in your hand!" The voice sank to a bitter whisper. "I *command* you, do you hear, you miserable slut! Do as you are told."

"No!" Ellen's voice quavered.

There was the sharp sound of a blow, and a whimper.

All in an instant Vernon Grove was off the sofa, grabbing the long bony wrist, twisting it till the revolver fell to the floor with a soft thud. He was grappling with the tall ungainly body, struggling with it not as man against man, but merely holding it and pinioning it, down, down, forcing it down upon the yellow sofa, hearing its wild curses and its obscene screams. For he knew now that he was not fighting a man, had known the minute she dropped her accent that he had been brought to bay by the only person in the world who might have witnessed the death scene in the castle—Maida's "friend" and voice coach, a brilliant actress who had herself planned a rendezvous, perhaps a final showdown, with Maida that night at Glyn Tower.

Josephine Ludlow's turban and spectacles had fallen off. Her hair was short and iron-gray. But those eyes—the hate in them was unmistakable.

"Bastard!" She beat her fists; she sobbed into the yellow cushions.

The fire crackled. Ellen stood at the hearth watching the blue flames lick at the cartridge, already reducing it to ash.

He picked up the revolver, emptied the bullets from it, and tossed the gun at Josephine Ludlow's feet. Then in silence he left, slamming the door behind him and walking down the red-carpeted stairs whence he had come, and out into the rainy foggy night.

He had gone perhaps two or three blocks when he heard a voice calling his name through the mist and fog.

"V-Vernon—"

He stopped and waited, while Ellen, white-faced, hatless, in her loose tan coat, appeared out of the mist.

"Take me with you, Vernon. P-please take me with you." Her teeth were chattering.

He started walking again, and she linked her arm through his. In the yellow aureole of a street lamp her face was pale, with a livid streak across her cheek.

"Please take me with you b-back to the ship, V-Vernon."

In the silence there was only the sound of their feet moving swiftly over the wet pavements.

"Please, Vernon . . . ?"

"I'm not going back to the ship, Ellen. I'm going to the police," he said at last.

"To confess, Vernon? After all this t-time?"

"Yes," he said. "After all this time."

She found his hand and pressed it.

In the cab she huddled close to him.

"Is there any hope for . . . um . . . us, Vernon?"

He kissed her sadly, gently. And in her answering kiss he felt all the passion, the tragedy, the despair and the hunger of a beautiful lost child. And the promise . . .

LUCILLE FLETCHER is famous for her unforgettable *Sorry, Wrong Number*, originally a radio show, later a novel, and finally a motion picture, for which she herself wrote the screen play. She has also written many syndicated short shorts and other scripts for radio, television and movies, and several novels.

She was born in Brooklyn, educated in public schools there, and took a B.A. degree at Vassar. She is married and lives in Oxford, Maryland.

F/FLE   Fletcher, Lucille
        THE GIRL IN CABIN B54

                77-5186

F/F   13138   Lucille

        THE GIRL IN CABIN B54

                77-5186

DATE	ISSUED TO
JAN 18 '78	Martha Graham
Nov 30	Betty Fryer
March 8	Debbie Knight
Mar 25	Judy Steille En